# Raves for Stephen King's
# THE COLORADO KID!

"[A] charming story…Mr. King has shown us a magic trick, an illusion, but, unlike most mystery writers, doesn't show us how it was done."
—*Otto Penzler, New York Sun*

"A riveting tale."
—*U.S. News & World Report*

"*The Colorado Kid* is Stephen King's existential despair, his *Nausea* or *Waiting for Godot*."
—*Los Angeles Times*

"King appears to be fumbling in his tackle box when, in fact, he's already slipped the hook into our cheeks and is pulling us inexorably toward the bemusing, maddening… final page. If it's ironic that King delivered an experiment to people who celebrate the art of formula, that's OK. One of the reasons the pulps remain popular is that, behind those uniformly lurid painted covers, there always lurked a few writerly surprises."
—*Booklist*

"King has a unique way of completely redefining genres, and his homage to the pulp mystery—a kind of deconstruction of the traditional blueprint—is no different…*The Colorado Kid* is a must-read for mystery aficionados as well as all those who call themselves Stephen King fans. It's an unusual and thought-provoking addition to the author's already mammoth body of work… *The Colorado Kid* will have readers speculating until the very last page—and long afterward."
—*Barnes & Noble*

"Compelling reading: The author has a matchless narrative gift, and the characters are beautifully drawn."
—*Ellery Queen's Mystery Magazine*

"One of King's best works to date...a small story with a big heart that transcends genre."
—*The Magazine of Fantasy & Science Fiction*

"One of his most intriguing books...the way it ends makes you think more than you will with most other novels."
—*Napierville Sun*

"The ending comes as a most daring shock...I loved it."
—*The Guardian (UK)*

"Though the tale may end in ambiguity, the storytelling is powerful and has real effect and impact."
—*The Daily Camera*

"This is the best kind of Americana, true regional writing, a yarn told in the bumpy eloquence of small-town talk."
—*Ed Gorman*

"A showcase for King's trademark skills—making the mundane seem ominous, creating characters who leap off the page."
—*Charlotte Observer*

"An exercise in pure storytelling, and a commentary on the nature of closure [by] a storyteller at his peak."
—*Cemetery Dance*

"Filled with local color, memorable characters, and well-realized details…It's an almost-perverse touch that King's contribution to a publisher honoring genre fiction would end with a hard kick against genre conventions. But in its own way, it's an appropriate touch…finding death and mystery in a nice peaceful place where such things aren't supposed to happen. Now, as in the crime paperback's heyday, the message remains the same: Be watchful. Wherever you make your home, evil and temptation will follow."
— *The A.V. Club*

"[This] volume will speak to those who appreciate good storytelling…Quintessential King."
— *Library Journal*

"Time and again, King has surprised readers with his range…those in search of good characters, excellent dialogue and skillful writing will find all these in abundance in *The Colorado Kid*."
— *Newark Star Ledger*

"King's hard-boiled tour de force [is] a sparse but psychologically taut and layered thriller."
— *Tampa Tribune*

"A gem of storytelling…thought-provoking."
— *Lansing State Journal*

"A fascinating piece of narrative…King has yet again done something new."
— *Chicago Sun-Times*

"It's a measure of how good King's storytelling is—no news there—that he's given us a mystery without a solution and not made us feel as if we've been cheated."
—*New York Newsday*

"A really gripping book…readers who value storytelling are going to have a blast…Once again King has done things his way and succeeded."
—*Kansas City Star*

"There came a morning in the spring—April, it would have been—when they spied a man sitting out on Hammock Beach. You know, just on the outskirts of the village."

Stephanie knew it well.

"He was just sittin there with one hand in his lap and the other—the right one—lying on the sand. His face was waxy-white except for small purple patches on each cheek. His eyes were closed and Nancy said the lids were bluish. His lips also had a blue cast to them, and his neck, she said, had a kind of puffy look to it. His hair was sandy blond, cut short but not so short that a little of it couldn't flutter on his forehead when the wind blew, which it did pretty much constant.

"Nancy says, 'Mister, are you asleep? If you're asleep, you better wake up.'

"Johnny Gravlin says, 'He's not asleep, Nancy.'

"Johnny reached down—he had to steel himself to do it, he told me that years later—and shook the guy's shoulder. He said he knew for sure when he grabbed hold, because it didn't feel like a real shoulder at all under there but like a carving of one. He shook twice. First time, nothing happened. Second time, the guy's head fell over on his left shoulder and the guy slid off the litter basket that'd been holding him up and went down on his side. His head thumped on the sand. Nancy screamed and ran back to the road, fast as she could… He caught up to her and put his arm around her and said he was never so glad to feel live flesh underneath his arm. He told me he's never forgotten how it felt to grip that dead man's shoulder, how it felt like wood under that white shirt…"

# The
# COLORADO
# Kíd

### by **Stephen King**

A HARD CASE CRIME NOVEL

**A HARD CASE CRIME BOOK**
(HCC-013-1)
*First Hard Case Crime edition: May 2019*

Published by

Titan Books
A division of Titan Publishing Group Ltd
144 Southwark Street
London  SE1 0UP

in collaboration with Winterfall LLC

ISBN 978-1-78909-155-7

Design direction by Max Phillips
*www.maxphillips.net*

Typeset by Swordsmith Productions

Printed in the United States of America

*Visit us on the web at www.HardCaseCrime.com*

With *admiration, for* DAN J. MARLOWE,
*author of* The Name of the Game is Death:
*Hardest of the hardboiled.*

# THE BIRTH (AND REBIRTH) OF THE COLORADO KID

When I first heard the title, I had two thoughts: boxing story or western.

This was back in 2004. I'd first reached out to Stephen King early in the year (April 16th, my obsessive record-keeping reminds me), sending him some materials about a line of books called "Hard Case Crime" that a friend and I were creating. We hadn't published any books yet—our first titles wouldn't come out until September—but we had a couple in the can and we'd hired painters to paint some covers, and our goal was nothing less than to revive pulp fiction in all its lurid mid-century glory. Gorgeous dames in torn negligees, tough guys with guns and felt hats, action and excitement, doom and despair.

Our books were going to be paperbacks, and not 500-page doorstops either—the sort of slender volumes you could read in a sitting or two, maybe on the train heading to or from work or while waiting for your clothes to spin dry at the laundromat.

In terms of content, we'd publish stories written at high

velocity, typically by authors who had to keep one eye out for the bill collector as they pounded the typewriter keys. The books would be the sort that grabbed you by the throat on page one and didn't let go till a killer was unmasked or someone lay bleeding in a gutter a scant 200 pages later. We'd package up these old-fashioned yarns behind sexy covers, price 'em about the same as a movie ticket (just as, in the old days, you could get either a movie ticket or a paperback for a quarter), and sell them in bookstores, truckstops, newsstands, drugstores, and military PXs across the land.

An ambitious plan. A quixotic plan. Not to mince words, a crazy plan. What could possibly have made us think that anyone in 2004 would want books that looked like they'd been published (and in some cases actually *had* first been published) half a century earlier?

Well, all I can say in my own defense is that there was drinking involved. But somehow we'd found backing for the project and had a publisher lined up to print and distribute the things, so we were charging full-steam ahead.

The only problem was how to get readers to give our books a try. We wanted to give voice to a new generation of hardboiled writers and to revive the work of an earlier generation that had long since been forgotten, terrific writers from the 1940s and 50s like David Dodge and Day Keene and Wade Miller. But modern readers wouldn't be likely to pick up a book by an author they'd never heard of, even if the cover price was modest and the cover art made their knees tremble. And I thought, maybe there's a well-known writer out there who loves old-time pulp crime novels as much as we do and would be willing to write us a blurb that would help entice readers to give us a try.

So I wrote to Stephen King.

Why Stephen King? Well, I didn't know the man, but I knew he shared our passion for this sort of book. He'd said so publicly more than once. He'd gone on the record about his love for the paperback crime novels of writers like John D. MacDonald and Lawrence Block. Hell, he'd even named the evil pseudonym in his novel *The Dark Half* "George Stark" after Richard Stark, the dark half of one of the writers we were going to be reprinting, the great Donald E. Westlake.

So I wrote to Stephen King. And held my breath and crossed my fingers and told myself not to be surprised if I never heard back. The man was busy, after all, and had to get a ton of random inquiries from random people wanting random things. No reason to think ours would catch his eye.

Then about a month later I was minding my own business when a call came in from Steve's agent and long-time editor, Chuck Verrill. "Steve asked me to give you a call," he said. "He wanted me to let you know that he does not want to write you a blurb—"

"Of course," I said, "I understand completely. That's completely understandable."

"—because," Chuck went on, "he wants to write you a book instead."

I sat on the other end of the phone while this sank in and tried to sound cool, like this was the sort of phone call I got every day and twice on Fridays. But inside I was turning cartwheels.

To this day I don't remember what I said to Chuck. But I remember what he said to me. He said that the book would be called *The Colorado Kid*, and though it would contain a mystery, it wasn't necessarily a crime novel, certainly not a conventional one, and would not fall strictly within our genre.

And I remember thinking, *The Colorado Kid*, not strictly within our genre...?

It's gotta be a boxing story. Either that or a western.

As you'll see, *The Colorado Kid* is not a boxing story and it's not a western. It's not a hardboiled crime novel either, though it surely does present a "hard case"—perhaps the hardest we've had the privilege to publish, since at its core the mystery of the Colorado Kid is the mystery we all wrestle with in our real lives, the mystery of the unanswerable. *The Colorado Kid* is an unusual and ambitious book, a tale about frustration that some readers have found frustrating—to which I answer, *Yes, exactly, that's the whole point!*

It's also very much a part of the classical mystery tradition we set out to revive. On the back cover I wrote that the book had "echoes of Dashiell Hammett's *The Maltese Falcon*," a comment that won me some raised eyebrows from readers who went looking in vain for Sam Spade. No, there are no trenchcoated private eyes in *The Colorado Kid*—no dames in torn negligees either, though in the best pulp tradition we didn't let that stop us from sticking a real looker on the cover. But as I reminded my skeptical inter-locutors, in *The Maltese Falcon* Sam Spade tells the story of an assignment he had once to search for a man named Flitcraft, who left his office one day to go to lunch and van-ished—vanished, Spade says, "like a fist when you open your hand."

*The Colorado Kid* is Stephen King's take on the Flitcraft parable, and it's as chilling and heartbreaking a reminder as any I've read that our ordinary, orderly lives are just one small sideways step away from a world of violence and terror and tragedy, a world of darkness that we don't nor-mally want to think about but sometimes find ourselves brushing up against, all unwilling. And if that's not a noir story, I don't know what is.

That was 2004, when we were all a lot younger than we are today. When we published *The Colorado Kid* the following year, it really put Hard Case Crime on the map. I have no doubt—zero—that our little publishing imprint would no longer be around today if not for this act of generosity on the part of a man who owed us nothing, who chose to do us a kindness beyond any we deserved. The book reached hundreds of thousands of readers, and millions more heard about it thanks to coverage on television and in newspa-pers and magazines. (The Internet wasn't such a big thing back then. Twitter didn't exist yet, and Facebook had only recently been founded. My old friend Jeff Bezos had already dreamed up Amazon.com, though, and he helped us out when the time came to announce the book. The story behind *The Colorado Kid* is one of kindness all around.)

In 2007, Pete Crowther brought out a set of beautifully packaged collectible hardcover editions of the book through his imprint PS Publishing in the UK. Simon & Schuster published it in audiobook and ebook editions, and various publishing houses around the world brought it out in German, Italian, Hebrew, Dutch and many other languages. It deserved it. As I wrote to Steve the day after I first read the manuscript, it's not just a good story, it's an important one. And important stories ought to get out to as many readers as possible in as many formats as possible.

*The Colorado Kid* even made it to television—sort of. The month after the book was published, I began talking with a young TV producer named Adam Fratto about the possibility of creating a Hard Case Crime TV series, along the lines of the old *Alfred Hitchcock Presents*, where we'd adapt a different book each week. While that never got off the ground, the one book we kept coming back to was *The Colorado Kid*, and after a year of working on the project with TV writers Jim Dunn and Sam Ernst, Adam and his colleagues sold a script based on the book to ABC. Hollywood being Hollywood, that script never got filmed—but after a few years we eventually got the rights back, re-sold the show to SyFy, and in 2010 it debuted there under the name *Haven*.

*Haven* ran for five seasons between 2010 and 2015— well, six, kinda; the fifth was twice the length of any previous season—and many fine writers and actors and producers and behind-the-scenes folk put their heart and soul into it. I worked on all 78 episodes, providing detailed notes on every script and even writing two or three episodes myself. It was a thrill to fly to L.A. each season to help kick off the writer's room and to the seaside village of Chester in Nova Scotia to watch the filming. When my daughter was born at the end of 2010, Jim and Sam even named the femme fatale in Season 2 after her, as a present. So I have a lot of fond memories of *Haven*. But just how much of *The Colorado Kid* made it into the show? Not a whole lot. The two elderly newspapermen you're about to meet were in there (reimagined as brothers), but the young newspaper intern Stephanie McCann was not, replaced by what the TV world felt was sexier and more interesting, a beautiful FBI agent named Audrey Parker. She acquired two handsome male foils, a good boy (Nathan, the local lawman) and a bad boy (Duke, modern-day pirate and proprietor of the Grey Gull), neither of whom has any counterpart in the book. The island off the coast of Maine where the story takes place was changed to a mainland town and renamed. And over the course of the five (six?) seasons, the dead body on the beach that's at the center of the plot eventually got thoroughly explained, the very outcome the book resists so mightily. And, oh, the whole thing became heavily supernatural, something the book ostensibly isn't (though Steve did hint to me once that his own solution to the mystery might just possibly involve supernatural intervention).

Was the show good? At its best, yes—the evidence being that fans to this day still stream episodes online and write fanfiction in which Duke and Nathan realize their true love was for each other all along. But was it *The Colorado Kid*? Only very, very obliquely.

That might, incidentally, be one of the reasons Steve chose to let the paperback edition of the book go out of print a decade ago—while the show was on the air, it seems to me he might not have wanted fans to pick up the book and be frustrated to discover that Audrey, Nathan and Duke weren't in it. But it has now been several years since the show ended, and it felt to both of us like the time was right to bring *The Colorado Kid* back. Just as we did the first time, we're publishing it as a good old-fashioned paperback, with a suitably pulpy cover painting, and for good measure we're adding a generous helping of interior art besides. (Including two lovely pieces by the painter Kate Kelton—who, by the way, is also an actress, one of whose acting credits was the part of Jordan on *Haven*. Given enough time, everything comes full circle, doesn't it?)

And so, the Colorado Kid returns home. Not to Colorado, but to Hard Case Crime, where he was born.

Dutch, Hebrew...audio, television...hardcover, Kindle... this little story has been through a mighty number of incarnations, and surely this one won't be its last. But paperback was the first way anyone ever read the story of the Colorado Kid, and you can tell me I'm biased if you like, but I still think it's the best.

Some stories are meant to live between embossed leather covers, some to be told around a crackling campfire, some projected on a movie screen, larger than life, at 24 frames per second.

And some were born to be hauled around town in your pocket, the pages bowed and the spine cracked.

Go on: dive in. If you don't finish in one sitting, you have my permission to dog-ear the page when your laundry's dry or your train's pulling into the station. The Kid'll be waiting for you when you come back, teasing your curiosity and reminding you that sometimes the stories that don't answer all your questions are the ones you remember for a lifetime.

Charles Ardai
*New York City, 2019*

*THE COLORADO KID*

# 1

After deciding he would get nothing of interest from the two old men who comprised the entire staff of *The Weekly Islander*, the feature writer from the Boston *Globe* took a look at his watch, remarked that he could just make the one-thirty ferry back to the mainland if he hurried, thanked them for their time, dropped some money on the table-cloth, weighted it down with the salt shaker so the stiffish onshore breeze wouldn't blow it away, and hurried down the stone steps from the Grey Gull's patio dining area toward Bay Street and the little town below. Other than a few cursory gleeps at her breasts, he hardly noticed the young woman sitting between the two old men at all.

Once the *Globe* writer was gone, Vince Teague reached across the table and removed the bills—two fifties—from beneath the salt shaker. He tucked them into a flap pocket of his old but serviceable tweed jacket with a look of unmistakable satisfaction.

"What are you *doing*?" Stephanie McCann asked, knowing how much Vince enjoyed shocking what he called "her young bones" (how much they both did, really), but in this instance not able to keep the shock out of her voice.

"What does it look like?" Vince looked more satisfied than ever. With the money gone he smoothed down the flap over the pocket and took the last bite of his lobster roll. Then he patted his mouth with his paper napkin and deftly caught the departed *Globe* writer's plastic lobster bib when another, fresher gust of salt-scented breeze tried to carry it away. His hand was almost grotesquely gnarled with arthritis, but mighty quick for all that.

"It looks like you just took the money Mr. Hanratty left to pay for our lunch," Stephanie said.

"Ayuh, good eye there, Steff," Vince agreed, and winked one of his own at the other man sitting at the table. This was Dave Bowie, who looked roughly Vince Teague's age but was in fact twenty-five years younger. It was all a matter of the equipment you got in the lottery, was what Vince claimed; you ran it until it fell apart, patching it up as needed along the way, and he was sure that even to folks who lived a hundred years—as he hoped to do—it seemed like not much more than a summer afternoon in the end.

"But *why*?"

"Are you afraid I'm gonna stiff the Gull for the tab and stick Helen with it?" he asked her.

"No…who's Helen?"

"Helen Hafner, she who waited on us." Vince nodded across the patio where a slightly overweight woman of about forty was picking up dishes. "Because it's the policy of Jack Moody—who happens to own this fine eating establishment, and his father before him, if you care—"

"I do," she said.

David Bowie, *The Weekly Islander*'s managing editor for just shy of the years Helen Hafner had lived, leaned forward and put his pudgy hand over her young and pretty one. "I know you do," he said. "Vince does, too. That's why he's taking the long way around Robin Hood's barn to explain."

"Because school is in," she said, smiling.

"That's right," Dave said, "and what's nice for old guys like us?"

"You only have to bother teaching people who want to learn."

"That's right," Dave said, and leaned back. "That's nice." He wasn't wearing a suit-coat or sport-coat but an old green sweater. It was August and to Stephanie it seemed quite warm on the Gull's patio in spite of the onshore breeze, but she knew that both men felt the slightest chill. In Dave's case, this surprised her a little; he was only sixty-five and carrying an extra thirty pounds, at least. But although Vince Teague might look no more than seventy (and an agile seventy at that, in spite of his twisted hands), he had turned ninety earlier that summer and was as skinny as a rail. "A stuffed string" was what Mrs. Pinder, *The Islander*'s part-time secretary, called him. Usually with a disdainful sniff.

"The Grey Gull's policy is that the waitresses are responsible for the tabs their tables run up until those tabs are paid," Vince said. "Jack tells all the ladies that when they come in lookin for work, just so they can't come whining to him later on, sayin they didn't know that was part of the deal."

Stephanie surveyed the patio, which was still half-full even at twenty past one, and then looked into the main dining room, which overlooked Moose Cove. There almost every table was still taken, and she knew that from Memorial Day until the end of July, there would be a line outside until nearly three o'clock. Controlled bedlam, in other words. To expect every waitress to keep track of every single customer when she was busting her ass, carrying trays of steaming boiled lobsters and clams—

"That hardly seems..." She trailed off, wondering if these two old fellows, who'd probably been putting out their paper before such a thing as the minimum wage even existed, would laugh at her if she finished.

"*Fair* might be the word you're lookin for," Dave said dryly, and picked up a roll. It was the last one in the basket.

*Fair* came out *fay-yuh*, which more or less rhymed with *ayuh*, the Yankee word which seemed to mean both *yes* and *is that so*. Stephanie was from Cincinnati, Ohio, and when she had first come to Moose-Lookit Island to do an internship on *The Weekly Islander*, she had nearly despaired...which, in downeast lingo, also rhymed with *ayuh*. How could she learn anything when she could only understand one word in every seven? And if she kept asking them to repeat themselves, how long would it be before they decided she was a congenital idiot (which on Moose-Look was pronounced *ijit*, of course)?

She had been on the verge of quitting four days into a four-month University of Ohio postgrad program when Dave took her aside one afternoon and said, "Don't you quit on it, Steffi, it'll come to ya." And it had. Almost overnight, it seemed, the accent had clarified. It was as if she'd had a bubble in her ear which had suddenly, miraculously popped. She thought she could live here the rest of her life and never talk like them, but understand them? Ayuh, that much she could do, deah.

"Fair was the word," she agreed.

"One that hasn't ever been in Jack Moody's vocabulary, except in how it applies to the weather," Vince said, and then, with no change of tone, "Put that roll down, David Bowie, ain't you gettin fat, I swan, soo-ee, pig-pig-pig."

"Last time I looked, we wa'ant married," Dave said, and took another bite of his roll. "Can't you tell her what's on what passes for your mind without scoldin me?"

"Ain't he pert?" Vince said. "No one ever taught him not to talk with his mouth full, either." He hooked an arm over the back of his chair, and the breeze from the bright ocean blew his fine white hair back from his brow. "Steffi, Helen's got three kids from twelve to six and a husband that run off and left her. She don't want to leave the island, and she can make a go of it—just—waitressin at the Grey Gull because summers are a little fatter than the winters are lean. Do you follow that?"

"Yes, absolutely," Stephanie said, and just then the lady in question approached. Stephanie noticed that she was wearing heavy support hose that did not entirely conceal varicose veins, and that there were dark circles under her eyes.

"Vince, Dave," she said, and contented herself with just

a nod at the pretty third, whose name she did not know. "See your friend dashed off. For the ferry?"

"Yep," Dave said. "Discovered he had to get back down-Boston."

"Ayuh? All done here?"

"Oh, leave on a bit," Vince said, "but bring us a check when you like, Helen. Kids okay?"

Helen Hafner grimaced. "Jude fell out of his treehouse and broke his arm last week. Didn't he holler! Scared me bout to death!"

The two old men looked at each other...then laughed. They sobered quickly, looking ashamed, and Vince offered his sympathies, but it wouldn't do for Helen.

"Men can laugh," she told Stephanie with a tired, sardonic smile. "They *all* fell out of treehouses and broke their arms when they were boys, and they all remember what little pirates they were. What they don't remember is Ma gettin up in the middle of the night to give em their aspirin tablets. I'll bring you the check." She shuffled off in a pair of sneakers with rundown backs.

"She's a good soul," Dave said, having the grace to look slightly shamefaced.

"Yes, she is," Vince said, "and if we got the rough side of her tongue we probably deserved it. Meanwhile, here's the deal on this lunch, Steffi. I dunno what three lobster rolls, one lobster dinner with steamers, and four iced teas cost down there in Boston, but that feature writer must have forgot that up here we're livin at what an economist might call 'the source of supply' and so he dropped a hundred bucks on the table. If Helen brings us a check that says any more than fifty-five, I'll smile and kiss a pig. With me so far?"

"Yes, sure," Stephanie said.

"Now the way this works for that fella from the *Globe* is that he scratches *Lunch, Gray Gull, Moose-Lookit Island* and *Unexplained Mysteries Series* in his little Boston *Globe* expense book while he's ridin back to the mainland on the ferry, and if he's honest he writes one hundred bucks and if he's got a smidge of larceny in his soul, he writes a hundred and twenty and takes his girl to the movies on the extra. Got that?"

"Yes," Stephanie said, and looked at him with reproachful eyes as she drank the rest of her iced tea. "I think you're very cynical."

"No, if I was very cynical, I would have said a hundred and *thirty*, and for sure." This made Dave snort laughter. "In any case, he left a hundred, and that's at least thirty-five dollars too much, even with a twenty percent tip added in. So I took his money. When Helen brings the check, I'll sign it, because the *Islander* runs a tab here."

"And you'll tip more than twenty percent, I hope," Stephanie said, "given her situation at home."

"That's just where you're wrong," Vince said.

"I am? *Why* am I?"

He looked at her patiently. "Why do you think? Because I'm cheap? Yankee-tight?"

"No. I don't believe that any more than I think black men are lazy or Frenchmen think about sex all day long."

"Then put your brain to work. God gave you a good one."

Stephanie tried, and the two men watched her do it, interested.

"She'd see it as charity," Stephanie finally said.

Vince and Dave exchanged an amused glance.

"What?" Stephanie asked.

"Gettin a little close to lazy black men and sexy Frenchmen, ain'tcha, dear?" Dave asked, deliberately broadening his downeast accent into what was nearly a burlesque drawl. "Only now it's the proud Yankee woman that won't take charity."

Feeling that she was straying ever deeper into the sociological thickets, Stephanie said, "You mean she would take it. For her kids, if not for herself."

"The man who bought our lunch was from away," Vince said. "As far as Helen Hafner's concerned, folks from away just about got money fallin out of their...their wallets."

Amused at his sudden detour into delicacy on her account, Stephanie looked around, first at the patio area where they were sitting, then through the glass at the indoor seating area. And she saw an interesting thing. Many—perhaps even most—of the patrons out here in the breeze were locals, and so were most of the waitresses serving them. Inside were the summer people, the so-called "off-islanders," and the waitresses serving *them* were younger. Prettier, too, and also from away. Summer help. And all at once she understood. She had been wrong to put on her sociologist's hat. It was far simpler than that.

"The Grey Gull waitresses share tips, don't they?" she asked. "That's what it is."

Vince pointed a finger at her like a gun and said, "Bingo."

"So what do you do?"

"What I do," he said, "is tip fifteen percent when I sign the check and put forty dollars of that *Globe* fella's cash in Helen's pocket. She gets all of that, the paper doesn't get hurt, and what Uncle Sam don't know don't bother him."

"It's the way America does business," Dave said solemnly.

"And do you know what I like?" Vince Teague said, turning his face up into the sun. When he squinted his eyes closed against its brilliance, what seemed like a thousand wrinkles sprang into existence on his skin. They did not make him look his age, but they *did* make him look eighty.

"No, what?" Stephanie asked, amused.

"I like the way the money goes around and around, like clothes in a drier. I like watching it. And this time when the machine finally stops turning, the money finishes up here on Moosie where folks actually need it. Also, just to make it perfect, that city fellow *did* pay for our lunch, and he walked away with *nones*."

"Ran, actually," Dave said. "Had to make that boat, don'tcha know. Made me think of that Edna St. Vincent Millay poem. 'We were very tired, we were very merry, we went back and forth all night on the ferry.' That's not exactly it, but it's close."

"He wasn't very merry, but he'll be good and tired by the time he gets to his next stop," Vince said. "I think he mentioned Madawaska. Maybe he'll find some unexplained mysteries there. Why anyone'd want to live in such a place, for instance. Dave, help me out."

Stephanie believed there was a kind of telepathy between the two old men, rough but real. She'd seen several examples of it since coming to Moose-Lookit Island almost three months ago, and she saw another example of it now. Their waitress was returning, check in hand. Dave's back was to her, but Vince saw her coming and the younger man knew exactly what the *Islander*'s editor wanted. Dave reached into his back pocket, removed his wallet, removed two bills, folded them between his fingers, and passed them across the table. Helen arrived a moment later. Vince took the check from her with one gnarled hand. With the other he slipped the bills into the skirt pocket of her uniform.

"Thank you, darlin," he said.

"You sure you don't want dessert?" she asked. "There's Mac's chocolate cherry cake. It's not on the menu, but we've still got some."

"I'll pass. Steffi?"

She shook her head. So—with some regret—did Dave Bowie.

Helen favored (if that was the word) Vincent Teague with a look of dour judgment. "You could use fattening up, Vince."

"Jack Sprat and his wife, that's me n Dave," Vince said brightly.

"Ayuh." Helen glanced at Stephanie, and one of her tired eyes closed in a brief wink of surprising good humor. "You picked a pair, Missy," she said.

"They're all right," Stephanie said.

"Sure, and after this you'll probably go straight to the *New York Times*," Helen said. She picked up the plates, added, "I'll be back for the rest of the ridding-up," and sailed away.

"When she finds that forty dollars in her pocket," Stephanie said, "will she know who put it there?" She looked again at the patio, where perhaps two dozen customers were drinking coffee, iced tea, afternoon beers, or eating off-the-menu chocolate cherry cake. Not all looked capable of slipping forty dollars in cash into a waitress's pocket, but some of them did.

"Probably she will," Vince said, "but tell me something, Steffi."

"I will if I can."

"If she didn't know, would that make it illegal tender?"

"I don't know what you—"

"I think you do," he said. "Come on, let's get back to the paper. News won't wait."

# 2

Here was the thing Stephanie loved best about *The Weekly Islander*, the thing that still charmed her after three months spent mostly writing ads: on a clear afternoon you could walk six steps from your desk and have a gorgeous view of the Maine coast. All you had to do was walk onto the shaded deck that overlooked the reach and ran the length of the newspaper's barnlike building. It was true that the air smelled of fish and seaweed, but everything on Moose-Look smelled that way. You got used to it, Stephanie had discovered, and then a beautiful thing happened—after your nose dismissed that smell, it went and found it all over again, and the second time around, you fell in love with it.

On clear afternoons (like this one near the end of August), every house and dock and fishing-boat over there on the Tinnock side of the reach stood out brilliantly; she could read the SUNOCO on the side of a diesel pump and the *LeeLee Bett* on the hull of some haddock-jockey's bread-winner, beached for its turn-of-the-season scraping and painting. She could see a boy in shorts and a cut-off Patriots jersey fishing from the trash-littered shingle below Preston's Bar, and a thousand winks of sun glittering off the tin flashing of a hundred village roofs. And, between Tinnock

Village (which was actually a good-sized town) and Moose-Lookit Island, the sun shone on the bluest water she had ever seen. On days like this, she wondered how she would ever go back to the Midwest, or if she even could. And on days when the fog rolled in and the entire mainland world seemed to be cancelled and the rueful cry of the foghorn came and went like the voice of some ancient beast…why, then she wondered the same thing.

*You want to be careful, Steffi*, Dave had told her one day when he came on her, sitting out there on the deck with her yellow pad on her lap and a half-finished Arts 'N Things column scrawled there in her big backhand strokes. *Island living has a way of creeping into your blood, and once it gets there it's like malaria. It doesn't leave easily.*

Now, after turning on the lights (the sun had begun going the other way and the long room had begun to darken), she sat down at her desk and found her trusty legal pad with a new Arts 'N Things column on the top page. This one was pretty much interchangeable with any of half a dozen others she had so far turned in, but she looked at it with undeniable affection just the same. It was hers, after all, her work, writing she was getting paid for, and she had no doubt that people all over the *Islander*'s circulation area—which was quite large—actually read it.

Vince sat down behind his own desk with a small but audible grunt. It was followed by a crackling sound as he twisted first to the left and then to the right. He called this "settling his spine." Dave told him that he would someday paralyze himself from the neck down while "settling his spine," but Vince seemed singularly unworried by the possibility. Now he turned on his computer while his managing editor sat on the corner of his desk, produced a toothpick, and began using it to rummage in his upper plate.

"What's it going to be?" Dave asked while Vince waited for his computer to boot up. "Fire? Flood? Earthquake? Or the revolt of the multitudes?"

"I thought I'd start with Ellen Dunwoodie snapping off the fire hydrant on Beach Lane when the parking brake on her car let go. Then, once I'm properly warmed up, I thought I'd move on to a rewrite of my library editorial," Vince said, and cracked his knuckles.

Dave glanced over at Stephanie from his perch on the corner of Vince's desk. "First the back, then the knuckles," he said. "If he could learn how to play 'Dry Bones' on his ribcage, we could get him on *American Idol*."

"Always a critic," Vince said amiably, still waiting for his machine to boot up. "You know, Steff, there's something perverse about this. Here am I, ninety years old and ready for the cooling board, using a brand new Macintosh computer, and there you sit, twenty-two and gorgeous, fresh as a new peach, yet scrawling on a yellow legal pad like an old maid in a Victorian romance."

"I don't believe yellow legal pads had been invented in Victorian times," Stephanie said. She shuffled through the papers on her desk. When she had come to Moose-Look and *The Weekly Islander* in June, they had given her the smallest desk in the place—little more than a grade-schooler's desk,

really—away in the corner. In mid-July she had been pro-
moted to a bigger one in the middle of the room. This
pleased her, but the increased desk-space also afforded
more area for things to get lost in. Now she hunted around
until she found a bright pink circular. "Do either of you
know what organization profits from the Annual End-Of-
Summer Gernerd Farms Hayride, Picnic, and Dance, this
year featuring Little Jonna Jaye and the Straw Hill Boys?"

"That organization would be Sam Gernerd, his wife,
their five kids, and their various creditors," Vince said, and
his machine beeped. "I've been meaning to tell you, Steff,
you've done a swell job on that little column of yours."

"Yes, you have," Dave agreed. "We've gotten two dozen
letters, I guess, and the only bad one was from Mrs. Edina
Steen the Downeast Grammar Queen, and she's completely
mad."

"Nuttier than a fruitcake," Vince agreed.

Stephanie smiled, wondering at how rare it was once
you graduated from childhood—this feeling of perfect and
uncomplicated happiness. "Thank you," she said. "Thank
you both." And then: "Can I ask you something? Straight
up?"

Vince swiveled his chair around and looked at her.
"Anything under the sun, if it'll keep me away from Mrs.
Dunwoodie and the fire hydrant," he said.

"And me away from doing invoices," Dave said. "Although
I can't go home until they're finished."

"Don't you make that paperwork your boss!" Vince said.
"How many times have I told you?"

"Easy for you to say," Dave returned. "You haven't looked inside the *Islander* checkbook in ten years, I don't think, let alone carried it around."

Stephanie was determined not to let them be sidetracked —or to let them sidetrack her—into this old squabble. "Quit it, both of you."

They looked at her, surprised into silence.

"Dave, you pretty much told that Mr. Hanratty from the *Globe* that you and Vince have been working together on the *Islander* for forty years—"

"Ayuh—"

"—and you started it up in 1948, Vince."

"That's true," he said. "'Twas *The Weekly Shopper and Trading Post* until the summer of '48, just a free handout in the various island markets and the bigger stores on the mainland. I was young and bullheaded and awful lucky. That was when they had the big fires over in Tinnock and Hancock. Those fires…they didn't *make* the paper, I won't say that—although there were those who did at the time— but they give it a good runnin start, sure. It wasn't until 1956 that I had as many ads as I did in the summer of '48."

"So you guys have been on the job for over fifty years, and in all that time you've *never* come across a real unexplained mystery? Can that be true?"

Dave Bowie looked shocked. "We never said that!"

"Gorry, you were *there*!" Vince declared, equally scandalized.

For a moment they managed to hold these expressions, but when Stephanie McCann only continued to look from one to the other, prim as the schoolmarm in a John Ford Western, they couldn't go on. First Vince Teague's mouth began to quiver at one corner, and then Dave Bowie's eye began to twitch. They might still have been all right, but then they made the mistake of looking right at each other and a moment later they were laughing like the world's oldest pair of kids.

# 3

"You were the one who told him about the *Pretty Lisa*," Dave said to Vince when he had gotten hold of himself again. The *Pretty Lisa Cabot* was a fishing boat that had washed up on the shore of neighboring Smack Island in the nineteen-twenties with one dead crewman sprawled over the forward hold and the other five men gone. "How many times do you think Hanratty heard that one, up n down this part of the coast?"

"Oh, I dunno, how many places do you judge he stopped before he got here, dear?" Vince countered, and a moment later the two men were off again, bellowing laughter, Vince slapping has bony knee while Dave whacked the side of one plump thigh.

Stephanie watched them, frowning—not angry, not amused herself (well…a little), just trying to understand the source of their howling good humor. She herself had thought the story of the *Pretty Lisa Cabot* good enough for at least one in a series of eight articles on, ta-da, Unexplained Mysteries of New England, but she was neither stupid nor insensitive; she'd been perfectly aware that Mr. *Hanratty* hadn't thought it was good enough. And yes, she'd known from his face that he'd heard it before in his

*Globe*-funded wanderings up and down the coast between Boston and Moose-Look, and probably more than once.

Vince and Dave nodded when she advanced this idea. "Ayup," Dave said. "Hanratty may be from away, but that doesn't make him lazy or stupid. The mystery of the *Pretty Lisa*—the solution to which almost certainly has to do with gun-happy bootleggers running hooch down from Canada, although no one will ever know for sure—has been around for years. It's been written up in half a dozen books, not to mention both *Yankee* and *Downeast* magazines. And, say, Vince, didn't the *Globe*—?"

Vince was nodding. "Maybe. Seven, maybe nine years ago. Sunday supplement piece. Although it might have been the Providence *Journal*. I'm sure it was the Portland Sunday *Telegram* that did the piece on the Mormons that showed up over in Freeport and tried to sink a mine in the Desert of Maine..."

"And the 1951 Coast Lights get a big play in the newspapers almost every Halloween," Dave added cheerfully. "Not to mention the UFO websites."

"And a woman wrote a book last year on the poisonin's at that church picnic in Tashmore," Vince finished up. This was the last 'unexplained mystery' they had hauled out for the *Globe* reporter over lunch. This was just before Hanratty had decided he could make the one-thirty ferry, and in a way Stephanie guessed she now didn't blame him.

"So you were having him on," she said. "Teasing him with old stories."

"No, dear!" Vince said, this time sounding shocked for

real. (*Well, maybe*, Stephanie thought.) "Every one of those is a *bona fide* unsolved mystery of the New England coast —our part of it, even."

"We couldn't be sure he knew all those stories until we trotted em out," Dave said reasonably. "Not that it surprised us any that he did."

"Nope," Vince agreed. His eyes were bright. "Pretty old chestnuts, I would have to agree. But we got a nice lunch out of it, didn't we? And we got to watch the money go around and come out right where it should...partly in Helen Hafner's pocket."

"And those stories are really the only ones you know? Stories that have been chewed to a pulp in books and the big newspapers?"

Vince looked at Dave, his long-time cohort. "Did I say that?"

"Nope," Dave said. "And I don't believe I did, either."

"Well, what other unexplained mysteries *do* you know about? And why didn't you tell him?"

The two old men glanced at each other, and once again Stephanie McCann felt that telepathy at work. Vince gave a slight nod toward the door. Dave got up, crossed the brightly lit half of the long room (in the darker half hulked the big old-fashioned offset printing press that hadn't run in over seven years), and turned the sign hanging in the door from OPEN to CLOSED. Then he came back.

"Closed? In the middle of the day?" Stephanie asked, with the slightest touch of unease in her mind, if not in her voice.

"If someone comes by with news, they'll knock," Vince said, reasonably enough. "If it's big news, they'll hammer."

"And if downtown catches afire, we'll hear the whistle," Dave put in. "Come on out on the deck, Steffi. August sun's not to be missed—it doesn't last long."

She looked at Dave, then at Vince Teague, who was as mentally quick at ninety as he'd been at forty-five. She was convinced of it. "School's in?" she asked.

"That's right," Vince said, and although he was still smiling, she sensed he was serious. "And do you know what's nice for old guys like us?"

"You only have to teach people who want to learn."

"Ayuh. Do *you* want to learn, Steffi?"

"Yes." She spoke with no hesitation in spite of that odd inner unease.

"Then come out and sit," he said. "Come out and sit a little."

So she did.

# 4

The sun was warm, the air was cool, the breeze was sweet with salt and rich with the sound of bells and horns and lapping water. These were sounds she had come to love in only a space of weeks. The two men sat on either side of her, and although she didn't know it, both had more or less the same thought: *Age flanks beauty*. And there was nothing wrong with the thought, because both of them understood their intentions were perfectly solid. They understood how good she could be at the job, and how much she wanted to learn; all that pretty greed made you *want* to teach.

"So," Vince said when they were settled, "think about those stories we told Hanratty at lunch, Steffi—the *Lisa Cabot*, the Coast Lights, the Wandering Mormons, the Tashmore church poisonings that were never solved—and tell me what they have in common."

"They're *all* unsolved."

"Try doin a little better, dearheart," Dave said. "You disappoint me."

She glanced at him and saw he wasn't kidding. Well, that *was* pretty obvious, considering why Hanratty had blown them to lunch in the first place: the *Globe*'s eight-installment series (maybe even ten installments, Hanratty had said, if he could find enough peculiar stories), which the editorial staff hoped to run between September and Halloween. "They've all been done to death?"

"That's a little better," Vince said, "but you're still not breaking any new ground. Ask yourself this, youngster: *why* have they been done to death? Why does some New England paper drag up the Coast Lights at least once a year, along with a bunch of blurry photos taken over half a century ago? Why does some regional magazine like *Yankee* or *Coast* interview either Clayton Riggs or Ella Ferguson at least once a year, as if they were going to all at once jump up like Satan in silk britches and say something brand new?"

"I don't know who those people are," Stephanie said.

Vince clapped a hand to the back of his head. "Ayuh, more fool me. I keep forgettin you're from away."

"Should I take that as a compliment?"

"Could do; probably *should* do. Clayton Riggs and Ella Ferguson were the only two who drank the iced coffee that day at Tashmore Lake and didn't die of it. The Ferguson woman's all right, but Riggs is paralyzed all down the left side of his body."

"That's awful. And they keep interviewing them?"

"Ayuh. Fifteen years have rolled by, and I think everyone with half a brain knows that no one is ever going to be arrested for that crime—eight folks poisoned by the side of the lake, and six of em dead—but still Ferguson and Riggs show up in the press, lookin increasin'ly rickety:

'What Happened That Day?' and 'The Lakeside Horror' and...you get the idea. It's just another story folks like to hear, like 'Little Red Ridin Hood' or 'The Three Billy Goats' Gruff.' Question is...*why*?"

But Stephanie had leaped ahead. "There *is* something, isn't there?" she said. "Some story you didn't tell him. What is it?"

Again that look passed between them, and this time she couldn't come even close to reading the thought that went with it. They were sitting in identical lawn chairs, Stephanie with her hands on the arms of hers. Now Dave reached over and patted one of them. "We don't mind tellin you... do we, Vince?"

"Nah, guess not," Vince said, and once again all those wrinkles appeared as he smiled up into the sun.

"But if you want to ride the ferry, you have to bring tea for the tillerman. Have you ever heard that one?"

"Somewhere." She thought on one of her mom's old record albums, up in the attic.

"Okay," Dave said, "then answer the question. Hanratty didn't want those stories because they've been written to rags. Why have they been?"

She thought about it, and once again they let her. Once again took pleasure in watching her do it.

"Well," Stephanie said, at last, "I suppose people like stories that are good for a shiver or two on a winter night, especially if the lights are on and the fire's nice and warm. Stories about, you know, the unknown."

"How many unknown things per story, dear?" Vince

Teague asked. His voice was soft but his eyes were sharp.

She opened her mouth to say *As many as six, anyway*, thinking about the Church Picnic Poisoner, then closed it again. Six people had died that day on the shores of Tashmore Lake, but one whopper dose of poison had killed them all and she guessed that just one hand had administered it. She didn't know how many Coast Lights there had been, but had no doubt that folks thought of it as a single phenomenon. So—

"One?" she said, feeling like a contestant in the Final Jeopardy round. "One unknown thing per story?"

Vince pointed his finger at her, smiling more widely than ever, and Stephanie relaxed. This wasn't real school, and these two men wouldn't like her any less if she flubbed an answer, but she had come to want to please them in a way she had only wanted to please the very best of her high school and college teachers. The ones who were fierce in their commitments.

"The other thing is that folks have to believe in their hearts that there's a *musta-been* in there someplace, and they got a damn good idea what it is," Dave said. "Here's the *Pretty Lisa*, washed up on the rocks just south of Dingle Nook on Smack Island in 1926—"

"'27," Vince said.

"All right, '27, smarty-britches, and Teodore Riponeaux is still on board, but dead as a hake, and the other five are gone, and even though there's no sign of blood or a struggle, folks say *musta-been* pirates, so now there's stories about how they had a treasure map and found buried gold and the folks that were guarding it took the swag off them and who knows what-all else."

"Or they got fighting among themselves," Vince said. "That's always been a *Pretty Lisa* favorite. The point is, there are stories some folks tell and other folks like to hear, but Hanratty was wise enough to know his editor wouldn't fall for such reheated hash."

"In another ten years, maybe," Dave said. "Because sooner or later, everything old is new again. You might not believe that, Steffi, but it's actually true."

"I *do* believe it," she said, and thought: *Tea for the Tillerman, was that Al Stewart or Cat Stevens?*

"Then there's the Coast Lights," Vince said, "and I can tell you exactly what's always made that such a favorite. There's a picture of them—probably nothing but reflected lights from Ellsworth on the low clouds that hung together just right to make circles that looked like saucers—and below them you can see the whole Hancock Lumber Little League team looking up, all in their uniforms."

"And one little boy pointin with his glove," Dave said. "It's the final touch. And people all look at it and say, 'Why, that *musta-been* folks from outer space, droppin down for a little look-see at the Great American Pastime. But it's still just one unknown thing, this time with interestin pictures to mull over, so people go back to it again and again."

"But not the Boston *Globe*," Vince said, "although I sense that one might do in a pinch."

The two men laughed comfortably, as old friends will.

"So," Vince said, "we might know of an unexplained mystery or two—"

"I won't stick at that," Dave said. "We know of at least one for sure, darlin, but there isn't a single *musta-been* about it—"

"Well…the steak," Vince said, but he sounded doubtful.

"Oh, ayuh, but even *that's* a mystery, wouldn't you say?" Dave asked.

"Yah," Vince agreed, and now he didn't sound comfortable. Nor did he look it.

"You're confusing me," Stephanie said.

"Ayuh, the story of the Colorado Kid is a confusing tale, all right," Vince said, "which is why it wouldn't do for the Boston *Globe*, don'tcha know. Too many unknowns, to begin with. Not a single *musta-been* for another." He leaned forward, fixing her with his clear blue Yankee gaze. "You want to be a newswoman, don't you?"

"You know I do," Stephanie said, surprised.

"Well then, I'm going to tell you a secret almost every newspaper man and woman who's been at it awhile knows: in real life, the number of actual stories—those with beginnings, middles, and ends—are slim and none. But if you can give your readers just one unknown thing (two at the very outside), and then kick in what Dave Bowie there calls a *musta-been*, your reader will tell *himself* a story. Amazin, ain't it?

"Take the Church Picnic Poisonings. No one knows who killed those folks. What *is* known is that Rhoda Parks, the Tashmore Methodist Church secretary, and William Blakee, the Methodist Church *pastor*, had a brief affair six months before the poisonings. Blakee was married, and he broke it off. Are you with me?"

"Yes," Stephanie said.

"What's *also* known is that Rhoda Parks was despondent over the breakup, at least for awhile. Her sister said as much. A third thing that's known? Both Rhoda Parks and William Blakee drank that poisoned iced coffee at the picnic and died. So what's the *musta-been*? Quick as your life, Steffi."

"Rhoda must have poisoned the coffee to kill her lover for jilting her and then drank it herself to commit suicide. The other four—plus the ones who only got sick—were what-do-you-call-it, collateral damage."

Vince snapped his fingers. "Ayuh, that's the story people tell themselves. The newspapers and magazines never come right out and print it because they don't have to. They know that folks can connect the dots. What's against it? Quick as your life again."

But this time her life would have been forfeit, because Stephanie could come up with nothing against it. She was about to protest that she didn't know the case well enough to say when Dave got up, approached the porch rail, looked out over the reach toward Tinnock, and remarked mildly: "Six months seems a long time to wait, doesn't it?"

Stephanie said, "Didn't someone once say revenge is a dish best eaten cold?"

"Ayuh," Dave said, still perfectly mild, "but when you kill six people, that's more than just revenge. Not sayin it *couldn't* have been that way, just that it might have been some other. Just like the Coast Lights might have been reflections on the clouds…or somethin secret the Air Force was testin that got sent up from the air base in Bangor…or who knows, maybe it *was* little green men droppin in to see if the kids from Hancock Lumber could turn a double play against the ones from Tinnock Auto Body."

"Mostly what happens is people make up a story and stick with it," Vince said. "That's easy enough to do as long as there's only one unknown factor: one poisoner, one set of mystery lights, one boat run aground with most of her crew gone. But with the Colorado Kid there was nothing *but* unknown factors, and hence there was no story." He paused. "It was like a train running out of a fireplace or a bunch of horses' heads showing up one morning in the middle of your driveway. Not that grand, but every bit as strange. And things like that…" He shook his head. "Steffi, people don't like things like that. They don't *want* things like that. A wave is a pretty thing to look at when it breaks on the beach, but too many only make you seasick."

Stephanie looked out at the sparkling reach—plenty of waves there, but no big ones, not today—and considered this in silence.

"There's something else," Dave said, after a bit.

"What?" she asked.

"It's *ours*," he said, and with surprising force. She thought it was almost anger. "A guy from the *Globe*, a guy from away—he'd only muck it up. He wouldn't understand."

"Do you?" she asked.

"No," he said, sitting down again. "Nor do I have to, dear. On the subject of the Colorado Kid I'm a little like the Virgin Mary, after she gave birth to Jesus. The Bible says something like, 'But Mary kept silent, and pondered these things in her heart.' Sometimes, with mysteries, that's best."

"But you'll tell me?"

"Why, yes, ma'am!" He looked at her as if surprised; also—a little—as if awakening from a near-doze. "Because you're one of us. Isn't she, Vince?"

"Ayuh," Vince said. "You passed that test somewhere around midsummer."

"Did I?" Again she felt absurdly happy. "How? What test?"

Vince shook his head. "Can't say, dear. Only know that at some point it began to seem you were all right." He glanced at Dave, who nodded. Then he looked back at Stephanie. "All right," he said. "The story we didn't tell at lunch. Our very own unexplained mystery. The story of the Colorado Kid."

# 5

But it was Dave who actually began.

"Twenty-five years ago," he said, "back in '80, there were two kids who took the six-thirty ferry to school instead of the seven-thirty. They were on the Bayview Consolidated High School Track Team, and they were also boy and girl-friend. Once winter was over—and it doesn't ever last as long here on the coast as it does inland—they'd run cross-island, down along Hammock Beach to the main road, then on to Bay Street and the town dock. Do you see it, Steffi?"

She did. She saw the romance of it, as well. What she didn't see was what the "boy and girlfriend" did when they got to the Tinnock side of the reach. She knew that Moose-Look's dozen or so high-school-age kids almost always took the seven-thirty ferry, giving the ferryman—either Herbie Gosslin or Marcy Lagasse—their passes so they could be recorded with quick winks of the old laser-gun on the bar codes. Then, on the Tinnock side, a schoolbus would be waiting to take them the three miles to BCHS. She asked if the runners waited for the bus and Dave shook his head, smiling.

"Nawp, ran that side, too," he said. "Not holdin hands, but might as well have been; always side by side, Johnny Gravlin and Nancy Arnault. For a couple of years they were all but inseparable."

Stephanie sat up straighter in her chair. The John Gravlin she knew was Moose-Lookit Island's mayor, a gregarious man with a good word for everyone and an eye on the state senate in Augusta. His hairline was receding, his belly expanding. She tried to imagine him doing the greyhound thing—two miles a day on the island side of the reach, three more on the mainland side—and couldn't manage it.

"Ain't makin much progress with it, are ya, dear?" Vince asked.

"No," she admitted.

"Well, that's because you see Johnny Gravlin the soccer player, miler, Friday night practical joker and Saturday lover as *Mayor* John Gravlin, who happens to be the only political hop-toad in a small island pond. He goes up and down Bay Street shaking hands and grinning with that gold tooth flashing off to one side in his mouth, got a good word for everyone he meets, never forgets a name or which man drives a Ford pickup and which one is still getting along with his Dad's old International Harvester. He's a caricature right out of an old nineteen-forties movie about small-town hoop-de-doo politics and he's such a hick he don't even know it. He's got one jump left in him—hop, toad, hop—and once he gets to that Augusta lilypad he'll either be wise enough to stop or he'll try another hop and end up getting squashed."

"That is *so* cynical," Stephanie said, not without youth's admiration for the trait.

Vince shrugged his bony shoulders. "Hey, I'm a stereotype myself, dearie, only my movie's the one where the newspaper feller with the arm-garters on his shirt and the eyeshade on his forread gets to yell out 'Stop the presses!' in the last reel. My point is that Johnny was a different creature in those days—slim as a quill pen and quick as quicksilver. You would have called him a god, almost, except for those unfortunate buck teeth, which he has since had fixed.

"And she…in those skimpy little red shorts she wore… she was indeed a goddess." He paused. "As so many girls of seventeen surely are."

"Get your mind out of the gutter," Dave told him.

Vince looked surprised. "Ain't," he said. "Ain't a bit. It's in the clouds."

"If you say so," Dave said, "and I will admit she was a looker, all right. And an inch or two taller than Johnny, which may be why they broke up in the spring of their senior year. But back in '80 they were hot and heavy, and every day they'd run for the ferry on this side and then up Bayview Hill to the high school on the Tinnock side. There were bets on when Nancy would catch pregnant by him, but she never did; either he was awful polite or she was awful careful." He paused. "Or hell, maybe they were just a little more sophisticated than most island kids back then."

"I think it might've been the running," Vince said judiciously.

Stephanie said, "Back on message, please, both of you," and the men laughed.

"On message," Dave said, "there came a morning in the spring of 1980—April, it would have been—when they spied a man sitting out on Hammock Beach. You know, just on the outskirts of the village."

Stephanie knew it well. Hammock Beach was a lovely spot, if a little overpopulated with summer people. She couldn't imagine what it would be like after Labor Day, although she would get a chance to see; her internship ran through the 5th of October.

"Well, not exactly *sitting*," Dave amended. "Half-sprawling was how they both put it later on. He was up against one of those litter baskets, don't you know, and their bases are planted down in the sand to keep em from blowing away in a strong wind, but the man's weight had settled back against this one until the can was…" Dave held his hand up to the vertical, then tilted it.

"Until it was like the Leaning Tower of Pisa," Steffi said.

"You got it exactly. Also, he wa'ant hardly dressed for early mornin, with the thermometer readin maybe forty-two degrees and a fresh breeze off the water makin it feel more like *thirty*-two. He was wearin nice gray slacks and a white shirt. Loafers on his feet. No coat. No gloves.

"The youngsters didn't even discuss it. They just ran over to see if he was okay, and right away they knew he wasn't. Johnny said later that he knew the man was dead as soon as he saw his face and Nancy said the same thing, but of course they didn't want to admit it—would you? Without making sure?"

"No," Stephanie said.

"He was just sittin there (well...half-sprawlin there) with one hand in his lap and the other—the right one—lying on the sand. His face was waxy-white except for small purple patches on each cheek. His eyes were closed and Nancy said the lids were bluish. His lips also had a blue cast to them, and his neck, she said, had a kind of *puffy* look to it. His hair was sandy blond, cut short but not so short that a little of it couldn't flutter on his forehead when the wind blew, which it did pretty much constant.

"Nancy says, 'Mister, are you asleep? If you're asleep, you better wake up.'

"Johnny Gravlin says, 'He's not asleep, Nancy, and he's not unconscious, either. He's not breathing.'

"She said later she knew that, she'd seen it, but she didn't want to believe it. Accourse not, poor kid. So she says, 'Maybe he is. Maybe he is asleep. You can't always tell when a person's breathing. Shake him, Johnny, see if he won't wake up.'

"Johnny didn't want to, but he also didn't want to look like a chicken in front of his girlfriend, so he reached down—he had to steel himself to do it, he told me that years later after we'd had a couple of drinks down at the Breakers—and shook the guy's shoulder. He said he knew for sure when he grabbed hold, because it didn't feel like a real shoulder at all under there but like a carving of one. But he shook it all the same and said, 'Wake up, mister, wake up and—' He was gonna say *die right* but thought that wouldn't sound so good under the circumstances (thinkin a little bit like a politician even back then, maybe) and changed it to '—and smell the coffee!'

"He shook twice. First time, nothing happened. Second time, the guy's head fell over on his left shoulder—Johnny had been shakin the right one—and the guy slid off the litter basket that'd been holding him up and went down on his side. His head thumped on the sand. Nancy screamed and ran back to the road, fast as she could…which was fast, I can tell you. If she hadn't've stopped there, Johnny probably would've had to chase her all the way down to the end of Bay Street, and, I dunno, maybe right out to the end of Dock A. But she *did* stop and he caught up to her and put his arm around her and said he was never so glad to feel live flesh underneath his arm. He told me he's never forgotten how it felt to grip that dead man's shoulder, and how it felt like wood under that white shirt."

Dave stopped abruptly, and stood up. "I want a Coca-Cola out of the fridge," he said. "My throat's dry, and this is a long story. Anyone else want one?"

It turned out they all did, and since Stephanie was the one being entertained—if that was the word—she went after the drinks. When she came back, both of the old men were at the porch rail, looking out at the reach and the mainland on the far side. She joined them there, setting the old tin tray down on the wide rail and passing the drinks around.

"Where was I?" Dave asked, after he'd had a long sip of his.

"You know perfectly well where you were," Vince said. "At the part where our future mayor and Nancy Arnault, who's God knows where—probably California, the good ones always seem to finish up about as far from the Island as they can go without needing a passport—had found the Colorado Kid dead on Hammock Beach."

"Ayuh. Well, John was for the two of em runnin right to the nearest phone, which would have been the one outside the Public Library, and callin George Wournos, who was the Moose-Look constable in those days (long since gone to his reward, dear—ticker). Nancy had no problem with that, but she wanted Johnny to set 'the man' up again first. That's what she called him: 'the man.' Never 'the dead man' or 'the body,' always 'the man.'

"Johnny says, 'I don't think the police like you to move them, Nan.'

"Nancy says, 'You *already* moved him, I just want you to put him back where he was.'

"And *he* says, 'I only did it because you told me to.'

"To which *she* answers, '*Please*, Johnny, I can't bear to look at him that way and I can't bear to *think* of him that way.' Then she starts to cry, which of course seals the deal, and he goes back to where the body was, still bent at the waist like it was sitting but now with its left cheek lying on the sand.

"Johnny told me that night at the Breakers that he never could have done what she wanted if she hadn't been right

there watchin him and countin on him to do it, and you
know, I believe that's so. For a woman a man will do many
things that he'd turn his back on in an instant when alone;
things he'd back away from, nine times out of ten, even
when drunk and with a bunch of his friends egging him on.
Johnny said the closer he got to that man lying in the
sand—only lying there with his knees up, like he was sitting in an invisible chair—the more sure he was that those
closed eyes were going to open and the man was going to
make a snatch at him. Knowing that the man was dead
didn't take that feeling away, Johnny said, but only made it
worse. Still, in the end he got there, and he steeled himself, and he put his hands on those wooden shoulders, and
he sat the man back up again with his back against that
leaning litter basket. He said he got it in his mind that the
litter basket was going to fall over and make a bang, and
when it did he'd scream. But the basket didn't fall and he
didn't scream. I am convinced in my heart, Steffi, that we
poor humans are wired up to always think the worst is
gonna happen because it so rarely does. Then what's only
lousy seems okay—almost good, in fact—and we can cope
just fine."

"Do you really think so?"

"Oh yes, ma'am! In any case, Johnny started away, then
saw a pack of cigarettes that had fallen out on the sand. And
because the worst was over and it was only lousy, he was
able to pick em up—even reminding himself to tell George
Wournos what he'd done in case the State Police checked
for fingerprints and found his on the cellophane—and put

em back in the breast pocket of the dead man's white shirt. Then he went back to where Nancy was standing, hugging herself in her BCHS warmup jacket and dancing from foot to foot, probably cold in those skimpy shorts she was wearing. Although it was more than the cold she was feeling, accourse.

"In any case, she wasn't cold for long, because they ran down to the Public Library then, and I'll bet if anyone had had a stopwatch on em, it would have shown a record time for the half-mile, or close to it. Nancy had lots of quarters in the little change purse she carried in her warmup, and she was the one who called George Wournos, who was just then gettin dressed for work—he owned the Western Auto, which is now where the church ladies hold their bazaars."

Stephanie, who had covered several for Arts 'N Things, nodded.

"George asked her if she was sure the man was dead, and Nancy said yes. Then he asked her to put Johnny on, and he asked Johnny the same question. Johnny also said yes. He said he'd shaken the man and that he was stiff as a board. He told George about how the man had fallen over, and the cigarettes falling out of his pocket, and how he'd put em back in, thinking George might give him hell for that, but he never did. *Nobody* ever did. Not much like a mystery show on TV, was it?"

"Not so far," Stephanie said, thinking it *did* remind her just a teensy bit of a *Murder, She Wrote* episode she'd seen once. Only given the conversation which had prompted this story, she didn't think any Angela Lansbury figures

69

would be showing up to solve the mystery…although someone must have made *some* progress, Stephanie thought. Enough, at least, to know where the dead man had come from.

"George told Johnny that he and Nancy should hurry on back to the beach and wait for him," Dave said. "Told em to make sure no one else went close. Johnny said okay. George said, 'If you miss the seven-thirty ferry, John, I'll write you and your lady-friend an excuse-note.' Johnny said that was the last thing in the world he was worried about. Then he and Nancy Arnault went back up there to Hammock Beach, only jogging instead of all-out runnin this time."

Stephanie could understand that. From Hammock Beach to the edge of Moosie Village was downhill. Going the other way would have been a tougher run, especially when what you had to run on was mostly spent adrenaline.

"George Wournos, meanwhile," Vince said, "called Doc Robinson, over on Beach Lane." He paused, smiling remembrance. Or maybe just for effect. "Then he called me."

# 6

"A murder victim shows up on the island's only public beach and the local law calls the editor of the local newspaper?" Stephanie asked. "Boy, that really *isn't* like *Murder, She Wrote*."

"Life on the Maine coast is rarely like *Murder, She Wrote*," Dave said in his driest tone, "and back then we were pretty much what we are now, Steffi, especially when the summer folk are gone and it's just us chickens—all in it together. That doesn't make it anything romantic, just a kind of…I dunno, call it a sunshine policy. If everyone knows what there is to know, it stops a lot of tongues from a lot of useless wagging. And murder! Law! You're a little bit ahead of yourself there, ain'tcha?"

"Let her off the hook on that one," Vince said. "We put the idea in her head ourselves, talkin about the coffee poisonins over in Tashmore. Steffi, Chris Robinson delivered two of my children. My second wife—Arlette, who I married six years after Joanne died—was good friends with the Robinson family, even dated Chris's brother, Henry, when they were in school together. It was the way Dave says, but it was more than business."

He put his glass of soda (which he called "dope") on the railing and then spread his hands open to either side of his face in a gesture she found both charming and disarming. *I will hide nothing,* it said. "We're a clubby bunch out here. It's always been that way, and I think it always will be, because we'll never grow much bigger than we are now."

"Thank *God*," Dave growled. "No friggin Wal-Mart. Excuse me, Steffi."

She smiled and told him he was excused.

"In any case," Vince said, "I want you to take that idea of murder and set it aside, Steffi. Will you do that?"

"Yes."

"I think you'll find that, in the end, you can't take it off the table or put it all the way back on. That's the way it is with so many things about the Colorado Kid, and what makes it wrong for the Boston *Globe*. Not to mention *Yankee* and *Downeast* and *Coast*. It wasn't even right for *The Weekly Islander*, not really. We *reported* it, oh yes, because we're a newspaper and reporting is our job—I've got Ellen Dunwoodie and the fire hydrant to worry about, not to mention the little Lester boy going to Boston for a kidney transplant—if he lasts long enough, that is—and of course you need to tell folks about the End-Of-Summer Hayride and Dance out at Gernerd Farms, don'tcha?"

"Don't forget the picnic," Stephanie murmured. "It's all the pie you can eat, and folks will want to know that."

The two men laughed. Dave actually patted his chest with his hands to show she had "gotten off a good one," as island folk put it.

"Ayuh, dear!" Vince agreed, still smiling. "But some-times a thing happens, like two high school kids on their mornin run finding a dead body on the town's prettiest beach, and you say to yourself, 'There must be a *story* in that.' Not just reporting—what, why, when, where, and how, but a *story*—and then you discover there just *isn't*. That it's only a bunch of unconnected facts surrounding a *true* unexplained mystery. And that, dear, is what folks don't want. It upsets em. It's too many waves. It makes em seasick."

"Amen," Dave said. "Now why don't you tell the rest of it, while we've still got some sunshine?"

And Vince Teague did.

# 7

"We were in on it almost from the beginning—and by *we* I mean Dave and me, *The Weekly Islander*—although I didn't print what I was asked by George Wournos not to print. I had no problem with that, because there was nothing in that business that seemed to affect the island's welfare in any way. That's the sort of judgment call newspaper folk make all the time, Steffi—you'll make it yourself—and in time you get used to it. You just want to make sure you never get comfortable with it.

"The kids went back and guarded the body, not that there was a lot of guardin to be done; before George and Doc Robinson pulled up, they didn't see but four cars, all headed for town, and none of em slowed down when they saw a couple of teenagers joggin in place or doin stretchin exercises there by the little Hammock Beach parkin lot.

"When George and the Doc got there, they sent Johnny and Nancy on their way, and that's where they leave the story. Still curious, the way people are, but on the whole glad to go, I have no doubt. George parked his Ford in the lot, Doc grabbed his bag, and they walked out to where the man was sitting against that litter barrel. He

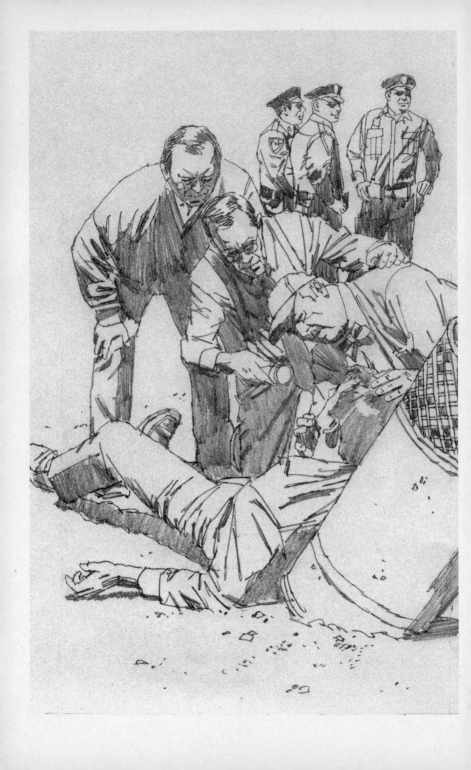

had slumped a little to one side again, and the first thing the Doc did was to haul him up nice and straight.

"'Is he dead, Doc?' George said.

"'Oh gorry, he's been dead at least four hours and probably six or more,' Doc says. (It was right about then that I came pulling in and parked my Chevy beside George's Ford.) 'He's as stiff as a board. *Rigor mortis.*'

"'So you think he's been here since…what? Midnight?' George asks.

"'He coulda been here since last Labor Day, for all I know,' Doc says, 'but the only thing I'm absolutely *sure* of is that he's been dead since two this morning. Because of the *rigor*. *Probably* he's been dead since midnight, but I'm no expert in stuff like that. If the wind was coming in stiff from offshore, that could have changed when the *rigor* set in—'

"'No wind at all last night,' I says, joining them. 'Calm as the inside of a churchbell.'

"'Well lookit here, another damn country heard from,' says Doc Robinson. 'Maybe you'd like to pronounce the time of death yourself, Jimmy Olsen.'

"'No,' I says, 'I'll leave that to you.'

"'I think I'll leave it to the County Medical Examiner,' he says. 'Cathcart, over in Tinnock. The state pays him an extra eleven grand a year for educated gut-tossin. Not enough, in my humble opinion, but each to his own. I'm just a GP. But…ayuh, this fella was dead by two, I'll say that much. Dead by the time the moon went down.'

"Then for maybe a minute the three of us just stood

there, looking down on him like mourners. A minute can be an awful short space of time under some circumstances, but it can be an awful long one at a time like that. I remember the sound of the wind—still light, but starting to build in a little from the east. When it comes that way and you're on the mainland side of the island, it makes such a lonely sound—"

"I know," Stephanie said quietly. "It kind of hoots."

They nodded. That in the winter it was sometimes a terrible sound, almost the cry of a bereft woman, was a thing she did not know, and there was no reason to tell her.

"At last—I think it was just for something to say—George asked Doc to take a guess as to how old the fella might be.

"'I'd put him right around forty, give or take five years,' he says. 'Do you think so, Vincent?' And I nodded. Forty seemed about right, and it occurred to me that it's too bad for a fella to die at forty, a real shame. It's a man's most anonymous age.

"Then the Doc seen something that interested him. He went down on one knee (which wasn't easy for a man of his size, he had to've gone two-eighty and didn't stand but five-foot-ten or so) and picked up the dead man's right hand, the one that'd been lying on the beach. The fingers were curled a little, as if he'd died trying to make them into a tube he could look through. When Doc held the hand up, we could see some grit stuck to the insides of the fingers and a little more dusted on the palm.

"'What do you see?' George asks. 'Doesn't look like anything but beach-sand to me.'

" 'That's all it is, but why's it sticking?' Doc Robinson asks back. 'This litter basket and all the others are planted well above the high-tide line, as anyone with half a brain would know, and there was no rain last night. Sand's dry as a bone. Also, look.'

"He picked up the dead man's left hand. We all observed that he was wearing a wedding ring, and also that there was no sand on his fingers or palm. Doc put that hand back down and picked up the other one again. He tipped it a little so the light shone better on the inside. 'There,' he says. 'Do you see?'

" 'What is that?' I ask. 'Grease? A little bit of grease?'

"He smiled and said, 'I think you win the teddy bear, Vincent. And see how his hand is curled?'

" 'Yuh—like he was playin spyglass,' George says. By then we was all three on our knees, as if that litter basket was an altar and we were tryin to pray the dead guy back to life.

" 'No, I don't think he was playing spyglass,' Doc says, and I realized somethin, Steffi—he was excited in the way people only are when they've figured something out they know the likes of them have no *business* figuring out in the ordinary course of things. He looked into the dead man's face (at least I thought it was his face Doc was lookin at, but it turned out to be a little lower than that), then back at the curled right hand. 'I don't think so at all,' he says.

" 'Then what?' George says. 'I want to get this reported to the State Police and the Attorney General's Office, Chris. What I *don't* want is to spend the mornin on my knees while you play Ellery Queen.'

"'See the way his thumb is almost touching his first finger and middle finger?' Doc asks us, and of course we did. 'If this guy had died looking through his rolled-up hand, his thumb would have been *over* his fingers, touching his middle finger and his third finger. Try it yourself, if you don't believe me.'

"I tried it, and I'll be damned if he wasn't right.

"'This isn't a tube,' Doc says, once again touching the dead man's stiff right hand with his own finger. 'This is a *pincers*. Combine that with the grease and those little bits of sand on the palm and the insides of the fingers, and what do you get?'

"I knew, but since George was the law, I let him say it. 'If he was eatin somethin when he died,' he says, 'where the hell is it?'

"Doc pointed to the dead man's neck—which even Nancy Arnault had noticed, and thought of as puffy—and he says, 'I've got an idea that most of it's still right in there where he choked on it. Hand me my bag, Vincent.'

"I handed it over. He tried rummaging through it and found he could only do it one-handed and still keep all that meat balanced on his knees: he was a big man, all right, and he needed to keep at least one hand on the ground to keep himself from tipping over. So he hands the bag over to me and says, 'I've got two otoscopes in there, Vincent—which is to say my little examination lights. There's my everyday and a spare that looks brand-new. We're going to want both of them.'

"'Now, now, I don't know about this,' George says. 'I

thought we were gonna leave all this for Cathcart, on the mainland. He's the guy the state hired for work like this.'

"'I'll take the responsibility,' Doc Robinson said. 'Curiosity killed the cat, you know, but satisfaction brought him back snap-ass happy. You got me out here in the cold and damp without my morning tea or even a slice of toast, and I intend to have a little satisfaction if I can. Maybe I won't be able to. But I have a feeling…Vincent, you take this one. George, you take the new one, and don't drop it in the sand, please and thank you, that's a two hundred-dollar item. Now, I haven't been down on all fours like a little kid playin horsie since I was I'm gonna say seven years old, and if I have to hold the position long I'm apt to fall on top of this fella, so you guys be quick and do just what I say. Have you ever seen how the folks in an art museum will train a couple of pin-spots on a small painting to make it look all bright and pretty?'

"George hadn't, so Doc Robinson explained. When he was done (and was sure George Wournos got it), the island's newspaper editor knelt on one side of that sittin-up corpse and the island's constable knelt on the other, each of us with one of the Doc's little barrel-lights in hand. Only instead of lighting up a work of art, we were going to light up the dead man's throat so Doc could take a look.

"He got himself into position with a fair amount of gruntin and puffing—woulda been funny if the circumstances hadn't been so strange, and if I hadn't been sort of afraid the man was going to have a heart-attack right there —and then he reached out one hand, slipped it into the guy's mouth, and hooked down his jaw like it was a hinge. Which, accourse, when you think about it, is just what it is.

"'Now,' he says. 'Get in close, boys. I don't think he's gonna bite, but if I'm wrong, I'll be the one who pays for the mistake.'

"We got in close and shone the lights down the dead man's gullet. It was just red and black in there, except for his tongue, which was pink. I could hear the Doc puffin and grunting and he says, not to us but to himself, 'A little more,' and he pulled down the lower jaw a little further. Then, to us, 'Lift em up, shine em straight down his gullet,' and we did the best we could. It changed the direction of the light just enough to take the pink off the dead man's tongue and put it on that hanging thing at the back of his mouth, the what-do-you-call-it—"

"Uvula," Stephanie and Dave said at the same time.

Vince nodded. "Ayuh, that. And just beyond it, I could see somethin, or the top of somethin, that was a dark gray. It was only for two or three seconds, but it was enough to satisfy Doc Robinson. He took his fingers out of the dead man's mouth—the lower lip made a kind of plopping sound as it went back against the gum, but the jaw stayed down pretty much where it was—and then he sat back, puffing away six licks to the dozen.

"'You boys are going to have to help me stand up,' he says when he got enough wind so he could talk. 'Both my legs are asleep from the knees on down. Damn, but I'm a fool to weigh this much.'

"'I'll help you up when you tell me,' George says. 'Did

you see anything? Because I didn't see anything. What about you, Vincent?'

"'I thought I did,' I says. The truth is I knew friggin well I did—pardon, Steff—but I didn't want to show him up.

"'Ayuh, it's back there, all right,' Doc says. He still sounded out of breath, but he sounded satisfied, too, like a man who's scratched a troublesome itch. 'Cathcart'll get it out and then we'll know if it's a piece of steak or a piece of pork or a piece of something else, but I don't see that it matters. We know what matters—he came out here with a piece of meat in his hand and sat down to eat it while he watched the moonlight on the reach. Propped his back up against this litter basket. And choked, just like the little Indian in the nursery rhyme. On the last bite of what he brought to snack on? Maybe, but not necessarily.'

"'Once he was dead, a gull could have swooped in and taken what was left right out of his hand,' George says. 'Just left the grease.'

"'Correct,' Doc says. 'Now are you two gonna help me up, or do I have to crawl back over to George's car and pull myself up by the doorhandle?'"

# 8

"So what do you think, Steffi?" Vince asked, taking a throat-cooling swallow of his Coke. "Mystery solved? Case closed?"

"Not on your granny!" she cried, and barely registered their appreciative laughter. Her eyes were sparkling. "The cause-of-death part, maybe, but…what *was* it, by the way? In his throat? Or would that be getting ahead of the story?"

"Darlin, you can't get ahead of a story that doesn't exist," Vince said, and his eyes were also sparkling. "Ask ahead, behind, or sideways. I'll answer anything. Same with Dave, I imagine."

As if to prove this was indeed so, *The Weekly Islander*'s managing editor said: "It was a piece of beef, probably steak, and very likely from one of your better cuts—your tenderloin, sirloin, or filet mignon. It was cooked medium-rare, and *asphyxiation due to choking* was what went on the death certificate, although the man we have always called the Colorado Kid also had suffered a massive cerebral embolism—your stroke, in other words. Cathcart decided the choking led to the stroking, but who knows, it might have been vicey-versa. So you see, even the cause of death gets slippery when you look at it right up close."

85

"There's at least one story in here—a little one—and I'm going to tell it to you now," Vince said. "It's about a fella who was in some ways like you, Stephanie, although I like to think you fell into better hands when it came to putting the final polish on your education; more compassionate ones, too. This fella was young—twenty-three, I think—and like you he was from away (the south in his case rather than the Midwest), and he was also doing graduate work, in the field of forensic science."

"So he was working with this Dr. Cathcart, and he figured something out."

Vince grinned. "Logical enough guess, dear, but you're wrong about who he was workin with. His name...what *was* his name, Dave?"

Dave Bowie, whose memory for names was as deadly as Annie Oakley's aim with her rifle, didn't hesitate. "Devane. Paul Devane."

"That's right, I recall it now you say it. This young man, Devane, was assigned to three months of post-graduate field work with a couple of State Police detectives out of the Attorney General's office. Only in his case, *sentenced* might be the better word. They treated him very badly." Vince's eyes darkened. "Older people who use young people badly when all the young people want is to learn—I think folks like that should be put out of their jobs. All too often, though, they get promotions instead of pink-slips. It has never surprised me that God gave the world a little tilt at the same time He set it spinning; so much that goes on here mimics that tilt.

"This young man, this Devane, spent four years at some place like Georgetown University, wanting to learn the sort of science that catches crooks, and right around the time he was coming to bud the luck of the draw sent him to work with a couple of doughnut-eating detectives who turned him into little more than a gofer, running files between Augusta and Waterville and shooing lookie-loos away from car-crash scenes. Oh, maybe once in awhile he got to measure a footprint or take flash photos of a tire-print as a reward. But rarely, I sh'd say. Rarely.

"In any case, Steffi, these two fine specimens of detec-tion—and I hope to God they're long out to pasture—hap-pened to be in Tinnock Village at the same time the body of the Colorado Kid turned up on Hammock Beach. They were investigating an apartment-house fire 'of suspicious origin,' as we say when reporting such things in the paper, and they had their pet boy, who was by then losing his idealism, with them.

"If he'd drawn a couple of the *good* detectives working out of the A.G.'s office—and I've met my share in spite of the goddam bureaucracy that makes so many problems in this state's law enforcement system—or if his Department of Forensic Studies had sent him to some other state that accepts students, he might have ended up one of the fellas you see on that *CSI* show—"

"I like that show," Dave said. "Much more realistic than *Murder, She Wrote*. Who's ready for a muffin? There's some in the pantry."

It turned out they all were, and story-time was suspended

until Dave brought them back, along with a roll of paper towels. When each of them had a Labree's squash muffin and a paper towel to catch the crumbs, Vince told Dave to take up the tale. "Because," he said, "I'm getting preachy and apt to keep us here until dark."

"I thought you was doin good," Dave said.

Vince clapped a bony hand to his even bonier chest. "Call 911, Steffi, my heart just stopped."

"That won't be so funny when it really happens, old-timer," Dave said.

"Lookit him spray those crumbs," Vince said. "You drool at one end of your life and dribble at t'other, my Ma used to say. Go on, Dave, tell on, but do us all a favor and swallow, first."

Dave did, and followed the swallow with a big gulp of Coke to wash everything down. Stephanie hoped her own digestive system would be up to such challenges when she reached David Bowie's age.

"Well," he said, "George didn't bother cordoning off the beach, because that just would have drawn folks like flies to a cowpie, don'tcha know, but that didn't stop those two dummies from the Attorney General's office from doin it. I asked one of em why they bothered, and he looked at me like I was a stark raving natural-born fool. 'Well, it's a crime scene, ain't it?' he says.

"'Maybe so and maybe no,' I says, 'but once the body's gone, what evidence do you think you're gonna have that the wind hasn't blown away?' Because by then that easterly had gotten up awful fresh. But they insisted, and I will admit it made a nice picture on the front page of the paper, didn't it, Vince?"

"Ayuh, picture with tape reading CRIME SCENE in it always sells copies," Vince agreed. Half of his muffin had already disappeared, and there were no crumbs Stephanie could see on his paper towel.

Dave said, "Devane was there while the Medical Examiner, Cathcart, got a look at the body: the hand with the sand on it, the hand with none, and then into the mouth, but right around the time the Tinnock Funeral Home hearse that had come over on the nine o'clock ferry pulled up, those two detectives realized he was still there and might be getting somethin perilously close to an education. They couldn't have that, so they sent him to get coffee and doughnuts and danishes for them and Cathcart and Cathcart's assistant and the two funeral home boys who'd just shown up.

"Devane didn't have any idea of where to go, and by then I was on the wrong side of the tape they'd strung, so I took him down to Jenny's Bakery myself. It took half an hour, maybe a little more, most of it spent ridin, and I got a pretty good idea of how the land lay with that young man, although I give him all points for discretion; he never told a single tale out of school, simply said he wasn't learning as much as he'd hoped to, and seeing the kind of errand he'd been sent on while Cathcart was doing his *in situ* examination, I could connect the dots.

"And when we got back the examination was over. The body had already been zipped away in a body-bag. That didn't stop one of those detectives—a big, beefy guy named

O'Shanny—from giving Devane the rough side of his tongue. 'What took you so long, we're freezin our butts off out here,' on and on, yatta-yatta-yatta.

"Devane stood up to it well—never complain, never explain, someone surely raised him right, I have to say—so I stepped in and said we'd gone and come back as fast as anyone could. I said, 'You wouldn't have wanted us to break any speed laws, now would you, officers?' Hoping to get a little laugh and kind of lighten the situation, you know. Didn't work, though. The other detective—his name was Morrison—said, 'Who asked you, Irving? Haven't you got a yard sale to cover, or something?' His partner got a laugh out of that one, at least, but the young man who was supposed to be learning forensic science and was instead learning that O'Shanny liked white coffee and Morrison took his black, blushed all the way down to his collar.

"Now, Steffi, a man doesn't get to the age I was even then without getting his ass kicked a number of times by fools with a little authority, but I felt terrible for Devane, who was embarrassed not only on his own account but on mine, as well. I could see him looking for some way to apologize to me, but before he could find it (or before I could tell him it wasn't necessary, since it wasn't him that had done anything wrong), O'Shanny took the tray of coffees and handed it to Morrison, then the two sacks of pastries from me. After that he told Devane to duck under the tape and take the evidence bag with the dead man's personal effects in it. 'You sign the Possession Slip,' he says to Devane, like he was talking to a five-year-old, 'and you make sure nobody else so much as touches it until I take it back from you. And keep your nose out of the stuff inside yourself. Have you got all that?'

"'Yes, sir,' Devane says, and he gives me a little smile. I watched him take the evidence bag, which actually looked like the sort of accordion-folder you see in some offices, from Dr. Cathcart's assistant. I saw him slide the Possession Slip out of the see-through envelope on the front, and…do you understand what that slip's for, Steffi?"

"I think I do," she said. "Isn't it so that if there's a criminal prosecution, and something found at the crime scene is used as evidence in that prosecution, the State can show an uncorrupted chain of possession from where that thing was found to where it finally ended up in some courtroom as Exhibit A?"

"Prettily put," Vince said. "You should be a writer."

"Very amusing," Stephanie said.

"Yes, ma'am, that's our Vincent, a regular Oscar Wilde," Dave said. "At least when he's not bein Oscar the Grouch. Anyway, I saw young Mr. Devane sign his name to the Possession Slip, and I saw him put it back into the sleeve on the front of the evidence bag. Then I saw him turn to watch those strongboys load the body into the funeral hack. Vince had already come back here to start writin his story, and that was when I left, too, telling the people who asked me questions—quite a few had gathered by then, drawn by that stupid yellow tape like ants to spilled sugar—that they could read all about it for just a quarter, which is what the *Islander* went for in those days.

"Anyway, that was the last time I actually saw Paul Devane, standing there and watchin those two widebodies load the dead man into the hearse. But I happen to know Devane disobeyed O'Shanny's order not to look in the evdence bag, because he called me at the *Islander* about sixteen months later. By then he'd given up his forensic science dream and gone back to school to become a lawyer. Good or bad, that particular course correction's down to A.G. Detectives O'Shanny and Morrison, but it was still Paul Devane who turned the Hammock Beach John Doe into the Colorado Kid, and eventually made it possible for the police to identify him."

"And we got the scoop," Vince said. "In large part because Dave Bowie here bought that young man a doughnut and gave him what money *can't* buy: an understanding ear and a little sympathy."

"Oh, that's layin it on a little thick," Dave said, shifting around in his seat. "I wa'nt with him more than thirty minutes. Maybe three-quarters of an hour if you want to add in the time we stood in line at the bakery."

"Sometimes maybe that's enough," Stephanie said.

Dave said, "Ayuh, sometimes maybe it is, and what's so wrong about that? How long do you think it takes a man to choke to death on a piece of meat, and then be dead forever?"

None of them had an answer to that. On the reach, some rich summer man's yacht tooted with hollow self-importance as it approached the Tinnock town dock.

# 9

"Let Paul Devane alone awhile," Vince said. "Dave can tell you the rest of that part in a few minutes. I think maybe I ought to tell you about the gut-tossing first."

"Ayuh," Dave said. "It ain't a story, Steff, but that part'd probably come next if it was."

Vince said, "Don't get the idea that Cathcart did the autopsy right away, because he didn't. There'd been two people killed in the apartment house fire that brought O'Shanny and Morrison to our neck of the woods to begin with, and they came first. Not just because they died first, but because they were murder victims and John Doe looked like being just an accident victim. By the time Cathcart *did* get to John Doe, the detectives were gone back to Augusta, and good riddance to them.

"I was there for that autopsy when it finally happened, because I was the closest thing there was to a professional photographer in the area back in those days, and they wanted a 'sleeping ID' of the guy. That's a European term, and all it means is a kind of portrait shot presentable enough to go into the newspapers. It's supposed to make the corpse look like he's actually snoozin."

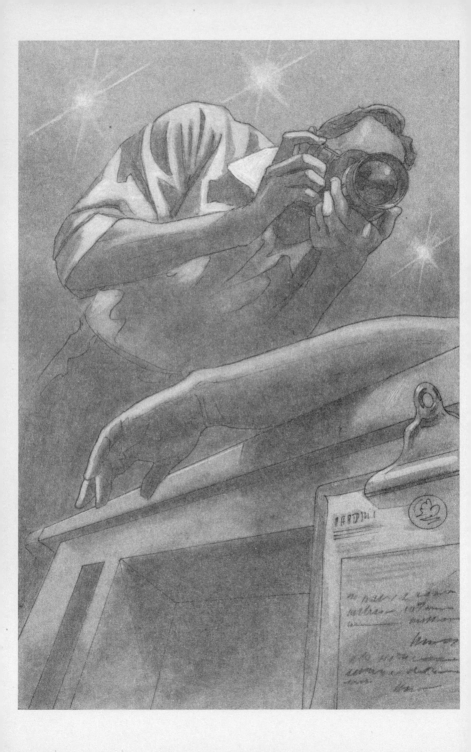

Stephanie looked both interested and appalled. "Does it work?"

"No," Vince said. Then: "Well...p'raps to a kid. Or if you was to look at it quick, and with one eye winked shut. This one had to be done before the autopsy, because Cathcart thought maybe, with the throat blockage and all, he might have to stretch the lower jaw too far."

"And you didn't think it would look quite so much like he was sleeping if he had a belt tied around his chin to keep his mouth shut?" Stephanie asked, smiling in spite of herself. It was awful that such a thing should be funny, but it *was* funny; some appalling creature in her mind insisted on popping up one sicko cartoon image after another.

"Nope, probably not," Vince agreed, and he was also smiling. Dave, too. So if she was sick, she wasn't the only one. Thank God. "What such a thing'd look like, I think, would be a corpse with a toothache."

Then they were all laughing. Stephanie thought that she loved these two old buzzards, she really did.

"Got to laugh at the Reaper," Vince said, plucking his glass of Coke off the railing. He helped himself to a sip, then put it back. "Especially when you're my age. I sense that bugger behind every door, and smell his breath on the pillow beside me where my wives used to lay their heads— God bless em both—when I put out my light.

"*Got* to laugh at the Reaper.

"Anyway, Steffi, I took my head-shots—my 'sleeping IDs'—and they came out about as you'd expect. The best one made the fella look like he mighta been sleepin off a bad drunk or was maybe in a coma, and that was the one we ran a week later. They also ran it in the Bangor *Daily News*, plus the Ellsworth and Portland papers. Didn't do any good, of course, not as far as scarin up people who knew him, at least, and we eventually found out there was a perfectly good reason for that.

"In the meantime, though, Cathcart went on about his business, and with those two dumbbells from Augusta gone back to where they came from, he had no objections to me hangin around, as long as I didn't put it in the paper that he'd let me. I said accourse I wouldn't, and accourse I never did.

"Working from the top down, there was first that plug of steak Doc Robinson had already seen in the guy's throat. 'That's your cause of death right there, Vince,' Cathcart said, and the cerebral embolism (which he discovered long after I'd left to catch the ferry back to Moosie) never changed his mind. He said that if the guy had had someone there to perform the Heimlich Maneuver—or if he'd per-formed it on himself—he might never have wound up on the steel table with the gutters running down the sides.

"Next, Contents of the Stomach Number One, and by that I mean the stuff on top, the midnight snack that had barely had a chance to start digesting when our man died and everything shut down. Just steak. Maybe six or seven bites in all, well-chewed. Cathcart thought maybe as much as four ounces.

"Finally, Contents of the Stomach Number Two, and here I'm talking about our man's supper. This stuff was pretty much—well, I don't want to go into details here; let's just say that the digestive process had gone on long enough so that all Dr. Cathcart could tell for sure without extensive testing was that the guy had had some sort of fish dinner, probably with a salad and french fries, around six or seven hours before he died.

"'I'm no Sherlock Holmes, Doc,' I says, 'but I can go you one better than that.'

"'Really?' he says, kinda skeptical.

"'Ayuh,' I says. 'I think he had his supper either at Curly's or Jan's Wharfside over here, or Yanko's on Moose-Look.'

"'Why one of those, when there's got to be fifty restaurants within a twenty-mile radius of where we're standin that sell fish dinners, even in April?' he asks. 'Why not the Grey Gull, for that matter?'

"'Because the Grey Gull would not stoop to selling fish and chips,' I says, 'and that's what this guy had.'

"Now Steffi—I'd done okay through most of the autopsy, but right about then I started feeling decidedly chuck-upsy. 'Those three places I mentioned sell fish and chips,' I says, 'and I could smell the vinegar as soon as you cut his stomach open.' Then I had to rush into his little bathroom and throw up.

"But I was right. I developed my 'sleeping ID' pictures that night and showed em around at the places that sold fish and chips the very next day. No one at Yanko's recognized him, but the take-out girl at Jan's Wharfside knew him right away. She said she served him a fish-and-chips basket, plus a Coke or a Diet Coke, she couldn't remember which, late on the afternoon before he was found. He took it to one of the tables and sat eating and looking out at the water. I asked if he said anything, and she said not really, just please and thank you. I asked if she noticed where he went when he finished his meal—which he ate around five-thirty—and she said no."

He looked at Stephanie. "My guess is probably down to the town dock, to catch the six o'clock ferry to Moosie. The time would have been just about right."

"Ayuh, that's what I've always figured," Dave said.

Stephanie sat up straight as something occurred to her. "It was April. The middle of April on the coast of Maine, but he had no coat on when he was found. Was he wearing a coat when he was served at Jan's?"

Both of the old men grinned at her as if she had just solved some complicated equation. Only, Stephanie knew, their business—even at the humble *Weekly Islander* level—was less about solving than it was delineating what *needed* to be solved.

"That's a good question," Vince said.

"Lovely question," Dave agreed.

"I was saving that part," Vince said, "but since there's no *story*, exactly, saving the good parts doesn't matter…and if you want answers, dear heart, the store is closed. The take-out girl at Jan's didn't remember for sure, and no one else remembered him at all. I suppose we have to count ourselves lucky, in a way; had he bellied up to that counter in mid-July, when such places have a million people in em, all wanting fish-and-chips baskets, lobster rolls, and ice cream sundaes, she wouldn't have remembered him at all unless he'd dropped his trousers and mooned her."

"Maybe not even then," Stephanie said.

"That's true. As it was, she *did* remember him, but not if he was wearing a coat. I didn't press her too hard on it, either, knowin that if I did she might remember somethin just to please me…or to get me out of her hair. She said 'I seem to recall he was wearing a light green jacket, Mr. Teague, but that could be wrong.' And maybe it *was* wrong, but do you know…I tend to think she was right. That he was wearing such a jacket."

"Then where was it?" Stephanie asked. "Did such a jacket ever turn up?"

"No," Dave said, "so maybe there *was* no jacket…although what he was doing outside on a raw seacoast night in April without one certainly beggars *my* imagination."

Stephanie turned back to Vince, suddenly with a thousand questions, all urgent, none fully articulated.

"What are you smiling about, dear?" Vince asked.

"I don't know." She paused. "Yes, I do. I have so god-damned many questions I don't know which one to ask first."

Both of the old men whooped at that one. Dave actually fished a big handkerchief out of his back pocket and mopped his eyes with it. "Ain't that a corker!" he exclaimed. "Yes, ma'am! I tell you what, Steff: why don't you pretend you're drawin for the Tupperware set at the Ladies Auxiliary Autumn Sale? Just close your eyes and pick one out of the goldfish bowl."

"All right," she said, and although she didn't quite do that, it was close. "What about the dead man's fingerprints? And his dental records? I thought that when it came to identifying dead people, those things were pretty much infallible."

"Most people do and probably they are," Vince said, "but you have to remember this was 1980, Steff." He was still smiling, but his eyes were serious. "Before the computer revolution, and *long* before the Internet, that marvelous tool young folks such as yourself take for granted. In 1980, you could check the prints and dental records of what police departments call an unsub—an unknown subject—against those of a person you thought your unsub might be, but checkin em against the prints or dental records of all the wanted felons on file in all the police departments would have taken years, and against those of all the folks reported disappeared every year in the United States? Even if you narrowed the list down to just men in their thirties and forties? Not possible, dear."

"But I thought the armed forces kept computer records, even back then…"

"I don't think so," Vince said. "And if they did, I don't believe the Kid's prints were ever sent to them."

"In any case, the initial ID didn't come from the man's fingerprints or dental work," Dave said. He laced his fingers over his considerable chest and appeared almost to preen in the day's late sunshine, now slanting but still warm. "I believe that's known as cuttin to the chase."

"So where *did* it come from?"

"That brings us back to Paul Devane," Vince said, "and I *like* coming back to Paul Devane, because, as I said, there's a story there, and stories are my business. They're my *beat*, we would have said back in the old, old days. Devane's a little sip of Horatio Alger, small but satisfying. *Strive and Succeed. Work and Win.*"

"*Piss and Vinegar*," Dave suggested.

"If you like," Vince said evenly. "Sure, ayuh, if you like. Devane goes off with those two stupid cops, O'Shanny and Morrison, as soon as Cathcart gives them the preliminary report on the burn victims from the apartment house fire, because they don't give a heck about some accidental choking victim who died over on Moose-Lookit Island. Cathcart, meanwhile, does his gut-tossing on John Doe with yours truly in attendance. Onto the death certificate goes *asphyxiation due to choking* or the medical equivalent thereof. Into the newspapers goes my 'sleeping ID' photo, which our Victorian ancestors much more truthfully called a 'death portrait.' And no one calls the Attorney General's Office or the State Police barracks in Augusta to say that's their missing father or uncle or brother.

"Tinnock Funeral Home keeps him in their cooler for six days—it's not the law, but like s'many things in matters of this sort, Steffi, you discover it's an accepted custom. Everybody in the death-business knows it, even if nobody knows *why*. At the end of that period, when he was still John Doe and still unclaimed, Abe Carvey went on ahead and embalmed him. He was put into the funeral home's own crypt at Seaview Cemetery—"

"This part's rather creepy," Stephanie said. She found she could see the man in there, for some reason not in a coffin (although he must surely have been provided with some sort of cheap box) but simply laid on a stone slab with a sheet over him. An unclaimed package in a post office of the dead.

"Ayuh, 'tis, a bit," Vince said levelly. "Do you want me to push on?"

"If you stop now, I'll kill you," she said.

He nodded, not smiling now but pleased with her just the same. She didn't know how she knew that, but she did.

"He boarded the summer and half the fall in there. Then, when November come around and the body was still un-named and unclaimed, they decided they ought to bury him." In Vince's Yankee accent, *bury* rhymed with *furry*. "Before the ground stiffened up again and made digging particularly hard, don't you see."

"I do," Stephanie said quietly. And she did. This time she didn't sense the telepathy between the two old men, but perhaps it was there, because Dave took up the tale (such tale as there was) with no prompting from the *Islander*'s senior editor.

"Devane finished out his tour with O'Shanny and Morrison to the bitter end," he said. "He probably even gave them each a tie or something at the end of his three months or his quarter or whatever it was; as I think I told you, Stephanie, there was no quit in that young fella. But as soon as he was finished, he put in his paperwork at whatever his college was—I *think* he told me Georgetown, but you mustn't hold me to that—and started back up again, taking whatever courses he needed for law school. And except for two things, that might have been where Mr. Paul Devane leaves this story—which, as Vince says, isn't a story at all, except maybe for this part. The first thing is that Devane peeked into the evidence bag at some point, and looked over John Doe's personal effects. The second is that he got serious about a girl, and she took him home to meet her parents, as girls often do when things get serious, and this girl's father had at least one bad habit that was more common then than it is now. He smoked cigarettes."

Stephanie's mind, which was a good one (both of the men knew this), at once flashed upon the pack of cigarettes that had fallen onto the sand of Hammock Beach when the dead man fell over. Johnny Gravlin (now Moose-Look's mayor) had picked it up and put it back into the dead man's pocket. And then something else came to her, not in a flash but in a blinding glare. She jerked as if stung. One of her feet struck the side of her glass and knocked it over. Coke fizzed across the weathered boards of the porch and dripped between them to the rocks and weeds far below. The old men didn't notice. They knew a state of grace perfectly well when they saw one, and were watching their intern with interest and delight.

*"The tax-stamp!"* she nearly shrieked. *"There's a state tax-stamp on the bottom of every pack!"*

They both applauded her, gently but sincerely.

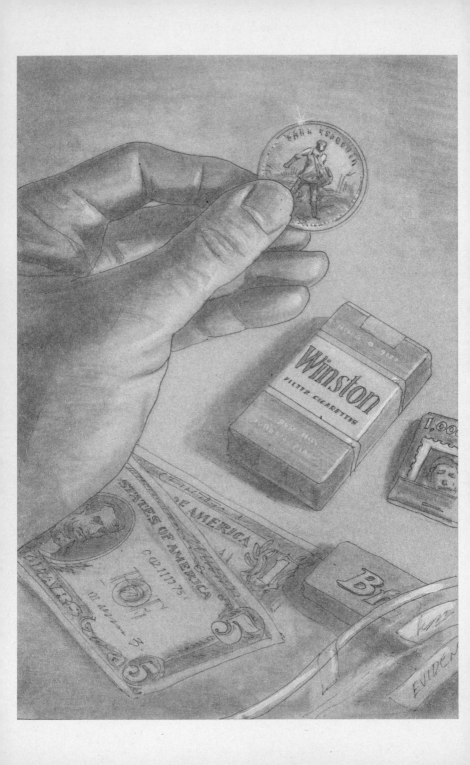

# 10

Dave said, "Let me tell you what young Mr. Devane saw when he took his forbidden peek into the evidence bag, Steffi—and I have no doubt he took that look more to spite those two than because he actually believed he'd see anything of value in such a scanty collection of stuff. To start with, there was John Doe's wedding ring; a plain gold band, no engraving, not even a date."

"They didn't leave it on his…" She saw the way the two men were looking at her, and it made her realize that what she was suggesting was foolish. If the man was identified, the ring would be returned. He might then be committed to the ground with it on his finger, if that was what his surviving family wanted. But until then it was evidence, and had to be treated as such.

"No," she said. "Of course not. Silly me. One thing, though—there must have been a Mrs. Doe somewhere. Or a Mrs. Kid. Yes?"

"Yes," Vince Teague said, rather heavily. "And we found her. Eventually."

"And were there little Does?" Stephanie asked, thinking that the man had been the right age for a whole gaggle of them.

"Let's not get stuck on that part of it just now, if you please," Dave said.

"Oh," Stephanie said. "Sorry."

"Nothing to be sorry about," he said, smiling a little. "Just don't want to lose m'place. It's easier to do when there's no… what would you call it, Vincent?"

"No through-line," Vince said. He was smiling, too, but his eyes were a little distant. Stephanie wondered if it was the thought of the little Does that had put that distance there.

"Nope, no through-line t'all," Dave said. He thought, then proved how little he'd lost his place by ticking items rapidly off on his fingers. "Contents of the bag was the deceased's weddin-ring, seventeen dollars in paper money —a ten, a five, and two ones—plus some assorted change that might have added up to a buck. Also, Devane said, one coin that wasn't American. He said he thought the writing on it was Russian."

"Russian," she marveled.

"What's called Cyrillic," Vince murmured.

Dave pressed ahead. "There was a roll of Certs and a pack of Big Red chewin gum with all but one stick gone. There was a book of matches with an ad for stamp-collectin on the front—I'm sure you've seen that kind, they hand em out at every convenience store—and Devane said he could see a strike-mark on the strip across the bottom for that purpose, pink and bright. And then there was that pack of cigarettes, open and with one or two cigarettes gone. Devane thought only one, and the single strike-mark on the matchbook seemed to bear that out, he said."

"But no wallet," Stephanie said.

"No, ma'am."

"And absolutely no identification."

"No."

"Did anyone theorize that maybe someone came along and stole Mr. Doe's last piece of steak *and* his wallet?" she asked, and a little giggle got out before she could put her hand over her mouth.

"Steffi, we tried that and everything else," Vince said. "Including the idea that maybe he got dropped off on Hammock Beach by one of the Coast Lights."

"Some sixteen months after Johnny Gravlin and Nancy Arnault found that fella," Dave resumed, "Paul Devane was invited to spend a weekend at his lady-friend's house in Pennsylvania. I have to think that Moose-Lookit Island, Hammock Beach, and John Doe were all about the last things on his mind just then. He said he and the girlfriend were going out for the evening, to a movie or somethin. Mother and Dad were in the kitchen, finishin the supper dishes—'doin the ridding-up' is what we say in these parts— and although Paul had offered to help, he'd been banished to the living room on the grounds of not knowin where anything went. So he was sittin there, watchin whatever was on the TV, and he happened to glance over at Poppa Bear's easy-chair, and there on Poppa Bear's little endtable, right next to Poppa Bear's *TV Guide* and Poppa Bear's ashtray, was Poppa Bear's pack of smokes."

He paused, giving her a smile and a shrug.

"It's funny how things work, sometimes; it makes you

wonder how often they *don't*. If that pack had been turned a different way—so the top had been facing him instead of the bottom—John Doe might have gone on being John Doe instead of first the Colorado Kid and then Mr. James Cogan of Nederland, a town just west of Boulder. But the bottom of the pack *was* facing him, and he saw the stamp on it. It was a *stamp*, like a postage stamp, and that made him think of the pack of cigarettes in the evidence bag that day.

"You see, Steffi, one of Paul Devane's minders—I disremember if it was O'Shanny or Morrison—had been a smoker, and among Paul's other chores, he'd bought this fella a fair smack of Camel cigarettes, and while they also had a stamp on them, it seemed to him it wasn't the same as the one on the pack in the evidence bag. It seemed to him that the stamp on the State of Maine cigarettes he bought for the detective was an *ink* stamp, like the kind you sometimes get on your hand when you go to a small-town dance, or...I dunno..."

"To the Gernerd Farms Hayride and Picnic?" she asked, smiling.

"You got it!" he said, pointing a plump finger at her like a gun. "Anyway, this wa'nt the kind of thing where you jump up yelling 'Eureka! I have found it!', but his mind kep' returnin to it over and over again that weekend, because the memory of those cigarettes in the evidence bag bothered him. For one thing, it seemed to Paul Devane that John Doe's cigarettes certainly *should* have had a Maine tax-stamp on them, no matter where he came from."

"Why?"

"Because there was only one gone. What kind of cigarette smoker only smokes one in six hours?"

"A light one?"

"A man who has a full pack and don't take but one cigarette out of it in six hours ain't a light smoker, that's a *non*-smoker," Vince said mildly. "Also, Devane saw the man's tongue. So did I—I was on my knees in front of him, shining Doc Robinson's otoscope into his mouth. It was as pink as peppermint candy. Not a smoker's tongue at all."

"Oh, and the matchbook," Stephanie said thoughtfully. "One strike?"

Vince Teague was smiling at her. Smiling and nodding. "One strike," he said.

"No lighter?"

"No lighter." Both men said it together, then laughed.

## 11

"Devane waited until Monday," Dave said, "and when the business about the cigarettes still wouldn't quit nagging him—wouldn't quit even though he was almost a year and a half downriver from that part of his life—he called me on the telephone and explained to me that he had an idea that maybe, just *maybe*, the pack of cigarettes John Doe had been carrying around hadn't come from the State of Maine. If not, the stamp on the bottom would show where they *had* come from. He voiced his doubts about whether John Doe was a smoker at all, but said the tax-stamp might be a clue even if he wasn't. I agreed with him, but was curious as to why he'd called me. He said he couldn't think of anyone else who still might be interested at that late date. He was right, I *was* still interested—Vince, too—and he turned out to be right about the stamp, as well.

"Now, I am not a smoker myself and never have been, which is probably one of the reasons I've attained the great age of sixty-five in such beautiful shape—"

Vince grunted and waved a hand at him. Dave continued, unperturbed.

"—so I made a little trip downstreet to Bayside News and asked if I could examine a package of cigarettes. My request was granted, and I observed that there was indeed an *ink* stamp on the bottom, not a postage-type stamp. I then made a call to the Attorney General's Office and spoke to a fellow name of Murray in a department called Evidence Storage and Filing. I was as diplomatic as I could possibly be, Stephanie, because at that time those two dumbbell detectives would still have been on active duty—"

"And they'd overlooked a potentially valuable clue, hadn't they?" Steff asked. "One that could have narrowed the search for John Doe down to one single state. And it was practically staring them in the face."

"Yep," Vince said, "and no way could they blame their intern, either, because they'd specifically told him to keep his nose out of the evidence bag. Plus, by the time it became clear that he'd disobeyed them—"

"—he was beyond their reach," she finished.

"You said it," Dave agreed. "But they wouldn't have gotten much of a scolding in any case. Remember, they had an actual murder investigation going over in Tinnock—manslaughter, two folks burned to death—and John Doe was just a choking victim."

"Still…" Stephanie looked doubtful.

"Still dumb, and you needn't be too polite to say it, you're among friends," Dave told her with a grin. "But the *Islander* had no in'trest in makin trouble for those two detectives. I made that clear to Murray, and I also made it clear that this wasn't a criminal matter; all I was doing was tryin my best to find out who the poor fella was, because someplace there were very likely people missin him and wantin to know what had befallen him. Murray said he'd have to get back to me on that, which I kinda expected, but I still had a bad afternoon, wonderin if maybe I should have played my cards a little different. I could have, you know; I could have had Doc Robinson make the call to Augusta, or maybe even talked Cathcart into doing it, but the idea of using either of them as a cat's paw kind of went against my grain. I s'pose it's corny, but I really do believe that in nine cases out of ten, honesty's the best policy. I was just worried this one might turn out to be the tenth.

"In the end, though, it came out all right. Murray called me back just after I'd made up my mind he wasn't going to and had started pullin on my jacket to go home for the day—isn't that the way things like that usually go?"

"A watched pot never boils," Vince said.

"My gosh, that's like poitry, give me a pad and a pencil so I can write it down," Dave said, grinning more widely than ever. The grin did more than take years off his face; it knocked them flying, and she could see the boy he had been. Then he grew serious once more, and the boy disappeared again.

"In big cities evidence gets lost all the time, I understand, but I guess Augusta's not that big yet, even if it is the state capital. Sergeant Murray had no trouble whatsoever finding the evidence bag with Paul Devane's signature on the Possession Slip; he said he had it ten minutes after we got done talking. The rest of the time that went by he was trying to get permission from the right person to let me know what was inside it…which he finally did. The cigarettes were Winstons, and the stamp on the bottom was just the way Paul Devane remembered: a regular little stick-on type that said COLORADO in tiny dark letters. Murray said he'd be turning the information over to the Attorney General's office, and they'd appreciate knowing 'in advance of publication' if we got anywhere in identifying the Colorado Kid. That's what he called him, so I guess you could say it was Sergeant Murray in the A.G.'s Evidence Storage and Filing Department who coined the phrase. He also said he hoped that if we *did* have any luck identifying the guy, that we'd note in our story that the A.G.'s office had been helpful. You know, I thought that was sort of sweet."

Stephanie leaned forward, eyes shining, totally absorbed. "So what did you do next? How did you proceed?"

Dave opened his mouth to reply, and Vince put a hand on the managing editor's burly shoulder to stop him before he could. "How do you *think* we proceeded, dear?"

"School is in?" she asked.

"'Tis," he said.

And because she saw by his eyes and the set of his mouth (more by the latter) that he was absolutely in earnest, she thought carefully before replying.

"You…made copies of the 'sleeping ID'—"

"Ayuh. We did."

"And then…mmm…you sent it with clippings to—how many Colorado papers?"

He smiled at her, nodded, gave her a thumbs-up. "Seventy-eight, Ms. McCann, and I don't know about Dave, but I was amazed at how cheap it had become to send out such a number of duplications, even back in 1981. Why, it couldn't have come to a hundred bucks total out-of-pocket expense, even with the postage."

"And of course we wrote it all off to the business," said Dave, who doubled as the *Islander*'s bookkeeper. "Every penny. As we had every right to do."

"How many of them ran it?"

*"Every frickin one!"* Vince said, and fetched his narrow thigh a vicious slap. "Ayuh! Even the Denver *Post* and the Rocky Mountain *News*! Because *then* there was only one peculiar thing about it and a *beautiful* through-line, don't you see?"

Stephanie nodded. Simple and beautiful. She did see.

Vince nodded back, absolutely beaming. "Unknown man, maybe from Colorado, found on an island beach in Maine, two thousand miles away! No mention of the steak stuck halfway down his gullet, no mention of the coat that might have gotten off Jimmy-Jesus-knows-where (or might not have been there at all), no mention of the Russian coin in his pocket! Just the Colorado Kid, your basic Unexplained Mystery, and so, sure, they *all* ran it, even the free ones that are mostly coupons."

"And two days after the Boulder newspaper ran it near the end of October 1981," Dave said, "I got a call from a woman named Arla Cogan. She lived in Nederland, a little way up in the mountains from Boulder, and her husband had disappeared in April of the previous year, leaving her and a son who had been six months old at the time of his disappearance. She said his name was James, and although she had no idea what he could possibly have been doing on an island off the coast of Maine, the photograph in the *Camera* looked a great deal like her husband. A great deal, indeed." He paused. "I guess she knew it was more than just a passin resemblance, because she got about that far and then began to cry."

# 12

Stephanie asked Dave to spell Mrs. Cogan's first name. In Dave Bowie's thick Maine accent, all she was hearing was a bunch of *a*-sounds with an *l* in the middle.

He did so, then said, "She didn't have his fingerprints—accourse not, poor left-behind thing—but she was able to give me the name of the dentist they used, and—"

"Wait, wait, wait," Stephanie said, putting her hand up like a traffic cop. "This man Cogan, what did he do for a living?"

"He was a commercial artist in a Denver advertising agency," Vince said. "I've seen some of his work since, and I'd have to say he was a pretty good one. He was never going to go nationwide, but if you wanted a quick picture for an advertising circular that showed a woman holdin a roll of toilet tissue up like she'd just caught herself a prize trout, Cogan was your man. He commuted to Denver twice a week, on Tuesdays and Wednesdays, for meetings and product conferences. The rest of the time he worked at home."

She switched her gaze back to Dave. "The dentist spoke to Cathcart, the Medical Examiner. Is that right?"

"You're hittin on all cyclinders, Steff. Cathcart didn't

have any X-rays of the Kid's dental work, he wasn't set up for that and saw no reason to send the corpse out to County Memorial where dental X-rays could have been taken, but he noted all the fillings, plus the two crowns. Everything matched. He then went on ahead and sent copies of the dead man's fingerprints to the Nederland Police, who got a tech from the Denver P.D. to go out to the Cogan residence and dust James Cogan's home office for prints. Mrs. Cogan—Arla—told the fingerprint man he wouldn't find anything, that she'd cleaned the whole works from stem to stern when she'd finally admitted to herself that her Jim wasn't coming back, that he'd either left her, which she could hardly believe, or that something awful had happened to him, which she was *coming* to believe.

"The fingerprint man said that if Cogan had spent 'a significant amount of time' in the room that had been his study, there would still be prints." Dave paused, sighed, ran a hand through what remained of his hair. "There were, and we knew for sure who John Doe, also known as the Colorado Kid, really was: James Cogan, age forty-two, of Nederland, Colorado, married to Arla Cogan, father of Michael Cogan, age six months at the time of his father's disappearance, age going on two years at the time of his father's identification."

Vince stood up and stretched with his fisted hands in the small of his back. "What do you say we go inside, people? It's commencing to get a tiny bit chilly out here, and there's a little more to tell."

# 13

They each took a turn at the rest room hidden in an alcove behind the old offset press that they no longer used (the paper was now printed in Ellsworth, and had been since '02). While Dave took his turn, Stephanie put on the Mr. Coffee. If the story-that-was-not-a-story went on another hour or so (and she had a feeling it might), they'd all be glad of a cup.

When they were reconvened, Dave sniffed in the direction of the little kitchenette and nodded approvingly. "I like a woman who hasn't decided the kitchen's a place of slavery just because she works for a livin."

"I feel absolutely the same way about a man," Stephanie said, and when he laughed and nodded (she had gotten off another good one, two in one afternoon, a record), she tilted her own head toward the huge old press. "*That* thing looks like a place of slavery to me," she said.

"It looks worse than it ever was," Vince said, "but the one before it was a horror. That one'd take your arm off if you weren't careful, and make a damn good snatch at it even if you were. Now where were we?"

"With the woman who'd just found out she was a widow," Stephanie said. "I presume she came to get the body?"

"Yep," Dave said.

"And did one of you fetch her here from the airport in Bangor?"

"What do you think, dear?"

It wasn't a question Stephanie had to mull over for very long. By late October or early November of 1981, the Colorado Kid would have been very old business to the State of Maine authorities…and as a choking victim, he had been very minor business to begin with. Just an unidentified dead body, really.

"Of course you did. You two were really the only friends she had in the state of Maine." This idea had the odd effect of making her realize that Arla Cogan had been (and, somewhere, almost certainly still was) a real person, and not just a chess-piece in an Agatha Christie whodunit or an episode of *Murder, She Wrote*.

"I went," Vince said, speaking softly. He sat forward in his chair, looking at his hands, which were clasped in a driftwood gnarl below his knees. "She wasn't what I expected, either. I had a picture built in my head, one based on a wrong idea. I should have known better. I've been in the newspaper business sixty-five years—as long as my partner in crime there's been alive, and he's no longer the gay blade he thinks he is—and in that length of time, I've seen my share of dead bodies. Most of em would put all that romantic poetry stuff—'I saw a maiden fair and still'—out of your head in damn short order. Dead bodies are ugly things indeed, by n large; many hardly look human at all anymore. But that wasn't true of the Colorado Kid. He looked almost good enough to be the subject of one of those romantic poimes by Mr. Poe. I photographed him before the autopsy, accourse, you have to remember that, and if you stared at the finished portrait for more'n a second or two, he still looked deader than hell (at least to me he did), but yes, there was something kinda handsome about him just the same, with his ashy cheeks and pale lips and that little touch of lavender on his eyelids."

"Brrr," Stephanie said, but she sort of knew what Vince was saying, and yes, it was a poem by Poe it called to mind. The one about the lost Lenore.

"Ayuh, sounds like true love t'me," Dave said, and got up to pour the coffee.

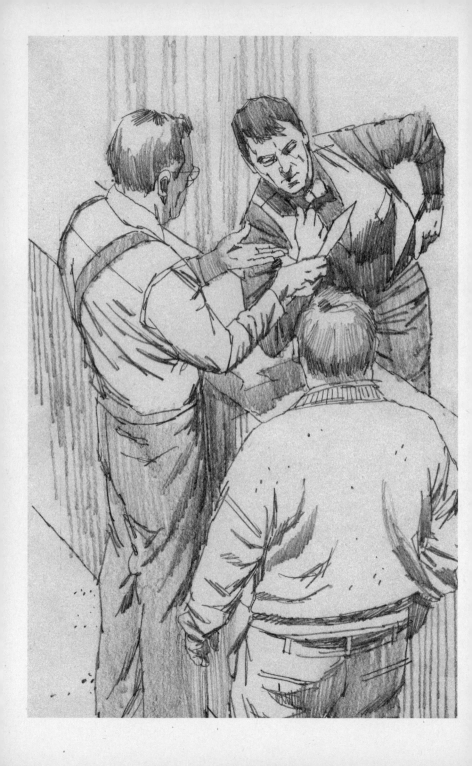

# 14

Vince Teague dumped what looked to Stephanie like half a carton of Half 'N Half into his, then went on. He did so with a rather rueful smile.

"All I'm trying to say is that I sort expected a pale and dark-haired beauty. What I got was a chubby redhead with a lot of freckles. I never doubted her grief and worry for a minute, but I sh'd guess she was one of those who eats rather than fasts when the rats gnaw at her nerves. Her folks had come from Omaha or Des Moines or somewhere to watch out for the baby, and I'll never forget how lost n somehow alone she looked when she came out of the jetway, holdin her little carry-on bag not by her side but up to her pouter-pigeon bosom. She wasn't a bit what I expected, not the lost Lenore—"

Stephanie jumped and thought, *Maybe now the telepathy goes three ways.*

"—but I knew who she was, right away. I waved and she came to me and said, 'Mr. Teague?' And when I said yes, that's who I was, she put down her bag and hugged me and said, 'Thank you for coming to meet me. Thank you for everything. I can't believe it's him, but when I look at the picture, I know it is.'

"It's a good long drive down here—no one knows that better than you, Steff—and we had lots of time to talk. The first thing she asked me was if I had any idea what Jim was doing on the coast of Maine. I told her I did not. Then she asked if he'd registered at a local motel on the Wednesday night—" He broke off and looked at Dave. "Am I right? Wednesday night?"

Dave nodded. "It would have been a Wednesday night she asked about, because it was a Thursday mornin Johnny and Nancy found him on. The 24th of April, 1980."

"You just *know* that," Stephanie marveled.

Dave shrugged. "Stuff like that sticks in my head," he told her, "and then I'll forget the loaf of bread I meant to bring home and have to go out in the rain and get it."

Stephanie turned back to Vince. "Surely he *didn't* register at a motel the night before he was found, or you guys wouldn't have spent so long calling him John Doe. You might have known him by some other alias, but no one registers at a motel under *that* name."

He was nodding long before she finished. "Dave and I spent three or four weeks after the Colorado Kid was found —in our spare time, accourse—canvassin motels in what Mr. Yeats would have called 'a widenin gyre' with Moose-Lookit Island at the center. It would've been damn near impossible during the summer season, when there's four hundred motels, inns, cabins, bed-and-breakfasts, and assorted rooms to rent all competing for trade within half a day's drive of the Tinnock Ferry, but it wasn't anything but a part-time job in April, because seventy percent of em are shut down from Thanksgiving to Memorial Day. We showed that picture everywhere, Steffi."

"No joy?"

"Not a bit of it," Dave confirmed.

She turned to Vince. "What did she say when you told her that?"

"Nothing. She was flummoxed." He paused. "Cried a little."

"Accourse she did, poor thing," Dave said.

"And what did you do?" Stephanie asked, all of her attention still fixed on Vince.

"My job," he said, with no hesitation.

"Because you're the one who always has to know," she said.

His bushy, tangled eyebrows went up. "Do you think so?"

"Yes," she said. "I do." And she looked at Dave for confirmation.

"I think she nailed you there, pard," Dave said.

"Question is, is it *your* job, Steffi?" Vince asked with a crooked smile. "*I* think it is."

"Sure," she said, almost carelessly. She had known this for weeks now, although if anyone had asked her before coming to the *Islander*, she would have laughed at the idea of deciding for sure on a life's work based on such an obscure posting. The Stephanie McCann who had almost decided on going to New Jersey instead of to Moose-Lookit off the coast of Maine now seemed like another person to her. A flatlander. "What did she tell you? What did she know?"

Vince said, "Just enough to make a strange story even stranger."

"Tell me."

"All right, but fair warning—this is where the through-line ends."

Stephanie didn't hesitate. "Tell me anyway."

# 15

"Jim Cogan went to work at Mountain Outlook Advertising in Denver on Wednesday, April the 23rd, 1980, just like any other Wednesday," Vince said. "That's what she told me. He had a portfolio of drawings he'd been working on for Sunset Chevrolet, one of the big local car companies that did a ton of print advertising with Mountain Outlook—a very valuable client. Cogan had been one of four artists on the Sunset Chevrolet account for the last three years, she said, and she was positive the company was happy with Jim's work, and the feeling was mutual—Jim liked working on the account. She said his specialty was what he called 'holy-shit women.' When I asked what that was, she smiled and said they were pretty ladies with wide eyes and open mouths, and usually with their hands clapped to their cheeks. The drawings were supposed to say, 'Holy shit, what a buy I got at Sunset Chevrolet!'"

Stephanie laughed. She had seen such drawings, usually in free advertising circulars at the Shop 'N Save across the reach, in Tinnock.

Vince was nodding. "Arla was a fair shake of an artist herself, only with words. What she showed me was a very decent man who loved his wife, his baby, and his work."

"Sometimes loving eyes don't see what they don't want to see," Stephanie remarked.

"Young but cynical!" Dave cried, not without relish.

"Well, ayuh, but she's got a point," Vince said. "Only thing is, sixteen months is usually long enough to put aside the rose-colored glasses. If there'd been something going on—discontent with the job or maybe a little honey on the side would seem the most likely—I think she would have found sign of it, or at least caught a whiff of it, unless the man was almighty, almighty careful, because during that sixteen months she talked to everyone he knew, most of em twice, and they all told her the same thing: he liked his job, he loved his wife, and he absolutely idolized his baby son. She kept coming back to that. 'He never would've left Michael,' she said. 'I know that, Mr. Teague. I know it in my soul.'" Vince shrugged, as if to say *So sue me*. "I believed her."

"And he wasn't tired of his job?" Stephanie asked. "Had no desire to move on?"

"She said not. Said he loved their place up in the mountains, even had a sign over the front door that said HER-NANDO'S HIDEAWAY. And she talked to one of the artists he worked with on the Sunset Chevrolet account, a fellow Cogan had worked with for years, Dave, do you recall that name—?"

"George Rankin or George Franklin," Dave said. "Cannot recall which, right off the top of my head."

"Don't let it get you down, old-timer," Vince said. "Even Willie Mays dropped a pop-up from time to time, I guess, especially toward the end of his career."

Dave stuck out his tongue.

Vince nodded as if such childishness was exactly what he'd come to expect of his managing editor, then took up the thread of his story once more. "George the Artist, be he Rankin or Franklin, told Arla that Jim had pretty much reached the top end of that which his talent was capable, and he was one of the fortunate people who not only knew his limitations but was content with them. He said Jim's remaining ambition was to someday head Mountain Outlook's art department. And, given that ambition, cutting and running for the New England coast on the spur of the moment is just about the last thing he would have done."

"But she thought that's what he *did* do," Stephanie said. "Isn't it?"

Vince put his coffee cup down and ran his hands through his fluff of white hair, which was already fairly crazy. "Arla Cogan's like all of us," he said, "a prisoner of the evidence.

"James Cogan left his home at 6:45 AM on that Wednesday to make the drive to Denver by way of the Boulder Turnpike. The only luggage he had was that portfolio I mentioned. He was wearing a gray suit, a white shirt, a red tie, and a gray overcoat. Oh, and black loafers on his feet."

"No green jacket?" Stephanie asked.

"No green jacket," Dave agreed, "but the gray slacks, white shirt, and black loafers were almost certainly what he was wearing when Johnny and Nancy found him sittin dead on the beach with his back against that litter basket."

"His suit-coat?"

"Never found," Dave said. "The tie, neither—but accourse if a man takes off his tie, nine times out of ten he'll stuff it into the pocket of his suit-coat, and I'd be willin to bet that if that gray suit-coat ever *did* turn up, the tie'd be in the pocket."

"He was at his office drawing board by 8:45 AM," Vince said, "working on a newspaper ad for King Sooper's."

"What—?"

"Supermarket chain, dear," Dave said.

"Around ten-fifteen," Vince went on, "George the Artist, be he Rankin or Franklin, saw our boy the Kid heading for the elevators. Cogan said he was goin around the corner to grab what he called 'a real coffee' at Starbucks and an egg salad sandwich for lunch, because he planned to eat at his desk. He asked George if George wanted anything."

"This is all what Arla told you when you were driving her out to Tinnock?"

"Yes, ma'am. Taking her to speak with Cathcart, make a formal identification of the photo—'This is my husband, this is James Cogan'—and then sign an exhumation order. He was waiting for us."

"All right. Sorry to interrupt. Go on."

"Don't be sorry for asking questions, Stephanie, asking questions is what reporters *do*. In any case, George the Artist—"

"Be he Rankin or Franklin," Dave put in helpfully.

"Ayuh, him—he told Cogan that he'd pass on the coffee, but he walked out to the elevator lobby with Cogan so they could talk a little bit about an upcoming retirement party for a fellow named Haverty, one of the agency's founders. The party was scheduled for mid-May, and George the Artist told Arla that her mister seemed excited and looking forward to it. They batted around ideas for a retirement gift until the elevator came, and then Cogan got on and told George the Artist they ought to talk about it some more at lunch and ask someone else—some woman they worked with—what *she* thought. George the Artist agreed that was a pretty good idea, Cogan gave him a little wave, the elevator doors slid closed, and that's the last person who can remember seeing the Colorado Kid when he was still in Colorado."

"George the Artist," she almost marveled. "Do you suppose any of this would have happened if George had said, 'Oh, wait a minute, I'll just pull on my coat and go around the corner with you?'"

"No way of telling," Vince said.

"Was *he* wearing his coat?" she asked. "Cogan? Was he wearing his gray overcoat when he went out?"

"Arla asked, but George the Artist didn't remember," Vince said. "The best he could do was say he didn't *think* so. And that's probably right. The Starbucks and the sandwich shop were side by side, and they really *were* right around the corner."

"She also said there was a receptionist," Dave put in, "but the receptionist didn't see the men go out to the elevators. Said she 'must have been away from her desk for a minute.'" He shook his head disapprovingly. "It's *never* that way in the mystery novels."

But Stephanie's mind had seized on something else, and it occurred to her that she had been picking at crumbs while there was a roast sitting on the table. She held up the forefinger of her left hand beside her left cheek. "George the Artist waves goodbye to Cogan—to the Colorado Kid—around ten-fifteen in the morning. Or maybe it's more like ten-twenty by the time the elevator actually comes and he gets on."

"Ayuh," Vince said. He was looking at her, bright-eyed. They both were.

Now Stephanie held up the forefinger of her right hand beside her right cheek. "And the counter-girl at Jan's Wharfside across the reach in Tinnock said he ate his fish-and-chips basket at a table looking out over the water at around five-thirty in the afternoon."

"Ayuh," Vince said again.

"What's the time difference between Maine and Colorado? An hour?"

"Two," Dave said.

"Two," she said, and paused, and said it again. "*Two.* So when George the Artist saw him for the last time, when those elevator doors slid shut, it was already past noon in Maine."

"Assuming the times are right," Dave agreed, "and assume's all we can do, isn't it?"

"Would it work?" she asked them. "Could he possibly have gotten here in that length of time?"

"Yes," Vince said.

"No," Dave said.

"Maybe," they said together, and Stephanie sat looking from one to the other, bewildered, her coffee cup forgotten in her hand.

# 16

"That's what makes this wrong for a newspaper like the *Globe*," Vince said, after a little pause to sip his milky coffee and collect his thoughts. "Even if we wanted to give it up."

"Which we don't," Dave put in (and rather testily).

"Which we don't," Vince agreed. "But if we did…Steffi, when a big-city newspaper like the *Globe* or the *New York Times* does a feature story or a feature series, they want to be able to provide *answers*, or at least suggest them, and do I have a problem with that? The hell I do! Pick up any big-city paper, and what do you find on the front page? Questions disguised as news stories. Where is Osama Bin Laden? We don't know. What's the President doing in the Middle East? *We* don't know because *he* don't. Is the economy going to get stronger or go in the tank? Experts differ. Are eggs good for you or bad for you? Depends on which study you read. You can't even get the weather forecasters to tell you if a nor'easter is going to come in from the nor'east, because they got burned on the last one. So if they do a feature story on better housing for minorities, they want to be able to say if you do A, B, C, and D, things'll be better by the year 2030."

"And if they do a feature story on Unexplained Mysteries,"

Dave said, "they want to be able to tell you the Coast Lights were reflections on the clouds, and the Church Picnic Poisonings were probably the work of a jilted Methodist secretary. But trying to deal with this business of the time…"

"Which you happen to have put your finger on," Vince added with a smile.

"And of course it's outrageous no matter *how* you think of it," Dave said.

"But I'm willing to be outrageous," Vince said. "Hell, I looked into the matter, just about dialed the phone off the damn wall, and I guess I have a right to be outrageous."

"My father used to say you can cut chalk all day, yet it won't never be cheese," Dave said, but he was also smiling a little.

"That's true, but let me whittle a little bit just the same," Vince said. "Let's say the elevator doors close at ten-twenty, Mountain Time, okay? Let's also say, just for the sake of argument, that this was all planned out in advance and he had a car standin by with the motor running."

"All right," Stephanie said, watching him closely.

"Pure fantasy," Dave snorted, but he also looked interested.

"It's farfetched, anyway," Vince agreed, "but he was *there* at quarter past ten and at Jan's Wharfside a little more than five hours later. That's also farfetched, but we know it's a fact. Now may I continue?"

"Have on, McDuff," Dave said.

"If he's got a car all warmed up and waiting for him, maybe he can make it to Stapleton in half an hour. Now he surely didn't take a commercial flight. He could have paid cash for his ticket and used an alias—that was possible back then—but there were no direct flights from Denver to Bangor. From Denver to anyplace in Maine, actually."

"You checked."

"I did. Flying commercial, the best he could have done was arrive in Bangor at 6:45 PM, which was long after that counter-girl saw him. In fact at that time of the year that's after the last ferry of the day leaves for Moosie."

"Six is the last?" Stephanie asked.

"Yep, right up until mid-May," Dave said.

"So he must have flown charter," she said. "A charter *jet*? Are there companies that flew charter jets out of Denver? And could he have afforded one?"

"Yes on all counts," Vince said, "but it would've cost him a couple of thousand bucks, and their bank account would have shown that kind of hit."

"It didn't?"

Vince shook his head. "There were no significant withdrawals prior to the fella's disappearance. All the same, that's what he must have done. I checked with a number of different charter companies, and they all told me that on a good day—one when the jet stream was flowing strong and a little Lear like a 35 or a 55 got up in the middle of it— that trip would take just three hours, maybe a little more."

"Denver to Bangor," she said.

"Denver to Bangor, ayuh—there's noplace closer to our part of the coast where one of those little burners can land. Not enough runway, don'tcha see."

She did. "So did you check with the charter companies in Denver?"

"I tried. Not much joy there, either, though. Of the five companies that flew jets of one size n another, only two'd even talk to me. They didn't have to, did they? I was just a small-town newspaperman lookin into an accidental death, not a cop investigating a crime. Also, one of em pointed out to me that it wasn't just a question of checking up on the FBOs that flew jets out of Stapleton—"

"What are FBOs?"

"Fixed Base Operators," Vince said. "Chartering aircraft is only one of the things they do. They get clearances, maintain little terminals for passengers who are flyin private so they can *stay* that way, they sell, service, and repair aircraft. You can go through U.S. Customs at lots of FBOs, buy an altimeter if yours is busted, or catch eight hours in the pilots' lounge if your current flyin time is maxed out. Some FBOs, like Signature Air, are big business—chain operations just like Holiday Inn or McDonald's. Others are seat-of-the-pants outfits with not much more than a coin-op snack machine inside and a wind-sock by the runway."

"You did some research," Stephanie said, impressed.

"Ayuh, enough to know that it isn't just Colorado pilots and Colorado planes that used Stapleton or any other Colorado airport, then or now. For instance, a plane from an FBO at LaGuardia in New York might fly into Denver with passengers who were going to spend a month in Colorado visiting relatives. The pilots would then ask around for passengers who wanted to go back to New York, just so they wouldn't have to make the return empty."

"Or these days they'd have their return passengers all set up ahead of time by computer," Dave said. "Do you see, Steff?"

She did. She saw something else as well. "So the records on Mr. Cogan's Wild Ride might be in the files of Air Eagle, out of New York."

"Or Air Eagle out of Montpelier, Vermont—" Vince said.

"Or Just Ducky Jets out of Washington, D.C.," Dave said.

"And if Cogan paid cash," Vince added, "there are quite likely no records at all."

"But surely there are all sorts of agencies—"

"Yes, ma'am," Dave said. "More than you could shake a stick at, beginning with the FAA and ending with the IRS. Wouldn't be surprised if the damn FFA wasn't in there somewhere. But in cash deals, paperwork gets thin. Remember Helen Hafner?"

Of course she did. Their waitress at the Grey Gull. The one whose son had recently fallen out of his treehouse and broken his arm. *She gets all of it,* Vince had said of the money he meant to put in Helen Hafner's pocket, *and what Uncle Sam don't know don't bother him.* To which Dave had added, *It's the way America does business.*

Stephanie supposed it was, but it was an extremely troublesome way of doing business in a case like this one.

"So you don't know," she said. "You tried your best, but you just don't know."

Vince looked first surprised, then amused. "As to tryin

my best, Stephanie, I don't think a person ever knows that for sure; in fact, I think most of us are condemned—damned, even!—to thinking we could have done just a little smidge better, even when we win through to whatever it was we were tryin to get. But you're wrong—I *do* know. He chartered a jet out of Stapleton. That's what happened."

"But you said—"

He leaned even further forward over his clasped hands, his eyes fixed on hers. "Listen carefully and take instruction, dearheart. It's long years since I read Sherlock Holmes, so I can't say this exactly, but at one point the great detective tells Dr. Watson somethin like this: 'When you eliminate the impossible, whatever is left—*no matter how improbable*—must be the answer.' Now we know that the Colorado Kid was in his Denver office buildin until ten-fifteen or ten-twenty on that Wednesday morning. And we can be pretty sure he was in Jan's Wharfside at five-thirty. Hold up your fingers like you did before, Stephanie."

She did as he asked, left forefinger for the Kid in Colorado, right forefinger for James Cogan in Maine. Vince unlocked his hands and touched her right forefinger briefly with one of his own, age meeting youth in midair.

"But don't call this finger five-thirty," he said. "We needn't trust the counter-girl, who wasn't run off her feet the way she would have been in July, but who was doubtless busy all the same, it bein the supper-hour and all."

Stephanie nodded. In this part of the world supper came early. Dinner—pronounced *dinnah*—was what you ate from your lunchpail at noon, often while out in your lobster boat.

"Let this finger be six o'clock," he said. "The time of the last ferry."

She nodded again. "He had to be on that one, didn't he?"

"He did unless he swam the reach," Dave said.

"Or chartered a boat," she said.

"We asked," Dave said. "More important, we asked Gard Edwick, who was the ferryman in the spring of '8o."

*Did Cogan bring him tea?* she suddenly found herself wondering. *Because if you want to ride the ferry, you're supposed to bring tea for the tillerman. You said so yourself, Dave. Or are the ferryman and the tillerman two different people?*

"Steff?" Vince sounded concerned. "Are you all right, dear?"

"I'm fine, why?"

"You looked…I dunno, like you came over strange."

"I sort of did. It's a strange story, isn't it?" And then she said, "Only it's not a story at all, you were so right about that, and if I came over strange, I suppose that's why. It's like trying to ride a bike across a tightrope that isn't there."

Stephanie hesitated, then decided to go on and make a complete fool of herself.

"Did Mr. Edwick remember Cogan because Cogan brought him something? Because he brought tea for the tillerman?"

For a moment neither man said anything, just regarded her with their inscrutable eyes—so strangely young and sweetly lad-like in their old faces—and she thought she might laugh or cry or do something, break out somehow just to kill her anxiety and growing certainty that she had made a fool of herself.

Vince said, "It was a chilly crossing. Someone—a man—brought a paper cup of coffee to the pilot house and handed it in to Gard. They only passed a few words. This was April, remember, and by then it was already going dark. The man said, 'Smooth crossing.' And Gard said, 'Ayuh.' Then the man said 'This has been a long time coming' or maybe 'I've been a long time coming.' Gard said it might have even been '*Lidle*'s been a long time coming.' There is such a name; there's none in the Tinnock phone book, but I've found it in quite a few others."

"Was Cogan wearing the green coat or the topcoat?"

"Steff," Vince said, "Gard not only didn't remember whether or not the man was wearing a coat; he probably couldn't have sworn in a court of law if the man was afoot or on hossback. It was gettin dark, for one thing; it was one little act of kindness and a few passed words recalled a year and a half downstream, for a second; for a third...well, old Gard, you know..." He made a bottle-tipping gesture.

"Speak no ill of the dead, but the man drank like a frickin fish," Dave said. "He lost the ferryman job in '85, and the Town put him on the plow, mostly so his family wouldn't starve. He had five kids, you know, and a wife with MS. But finally he cracked up the plow, doin Main Street while blotto, and put out all the frickin power for a frickin week in February, pardon my frickin *français*. Then he lost that job and he was on the town. So am I surprised he didn't remember more? No, I am not. But I'm convinced from what he *did* remember that, ayuh, the Colorado Kid came over from the mainland on the day's last ferry, and, ayuh, he brought tea for the tillerman, or a reasonable facsimile thereof. Good on you to remember about that, Steff." And he patted her hand. She smiled at him. It felt like a rather dazed smile.

"As you said," Vince resumed, "there's that two-hour time difference to factor in." He moved her left finger closer to her right. "It's quarter past twelve, east coast time, when Cogan leaves his office. He drops his easy-going, just-another-day act the minute the elevator doors open on the lobby of his building. The very *second*. He goes dashin outside, hellbent for election, where that fast car—and an equally fast driver—is waitin for him.

"Half an hour later, he's at a Stapleton FBO, and five minutes after that, he's mounting the steps of a private jet. He hasn't left this arrangement to chance, either. Can't have done. There are people who fly private on a fairly regular basis, then stay for a couple of weeks. The folks who take them one-way spend those two weeks attending to other charters. Our boy would have settled on one of those planes, and almost certainly would have made a cash arrangement to fly back out with them. Eastbound."

Stephanie said, "What would he have done if the people using the plane he planned to take cancelled their flight at the last minute?"

Dave shrugged. "Same thing he would've done if there

was bad weather, I guess," he said. "Put it off to another day."

Vince, meanwhile, had moved Stephanie's left finger a little further to the right. "Now it's getting close to one in the afternoon on the east coast," he said, "but at least our friend Cogan doesn't have to worry about a lot of security rigamarole, not back in 1980 and especially not flyin private. And we have to assume—again—that he doesn't have to wait in line with a lot of other planes for an active runway, because it screws up the timetable if he does, and all the while on the other end—" He touched her right finger. "—that ferry's waitin. Last one of the day.

"So, the flight lasts three hours. We'll say that, anyway. My colleague here got on the Internet, he loves that sucker with a passion, and he says the weather was good for flying that day and the maps show that the jet-stream was in approximately the right place—"

"But as to how *strong* it was, that's information I've never been able to pin down," Dave said. He glanced at Vince. "Given the tenuousness of your case, partner, that's probably not a real bad thing."

"We'll say three hours," Vince repeated, and moved Stephanie's left finger (the one she was coming to think of as her Colorado Kid finger) until it was less than two inches from her right one (which she now thought of as her James Cogan–Almost Dead finger). "It can't have been much longer than that."

"Because the facts won't let it," she murmured, fascinated (and, in truth, a little frightened) by the idea. Once, while in high school, she had read a science fiction novel called *The Moon Is A Harsh Mistress*. She didn't know about the moon, but she was coming to believe that was certainly true of time.

"No, ma'am, they won't," he agreed. "At four o'clock or maybe four-oh-five—we'll say four-oh-five—Cogan lands and disembarks at Twin City Civil Air, that was the only FBO at Bangor International Airport back then—"

"Any records of his arrival?" she asked. "Did you check?" Knowing he had, of course he had, also knowing it hadn't done any good, one way or another. It was that kind of story. The kind that's like a sneeze which threatens but never quite arrives.

Vince smiled. "Sure did, but in the carefree days before Homeland Security, all Twin City kept any length of time were their account books. They had a good many cash payments that day, includin some pretty good-sized refueling tabs late in the afternoon, but even those might mean nothing. For all we know, whoever flew the Kid in might have spent the night in a Bangor hotel and flown out the next morning—"

"Or spent the weekend," Dave said. "Then again, the pilot might have left right away, and without refueling at all."

"How could he do that, after coming all the way from Denver?" Stephanie asked.

"Could have hopped down to Portland," Dave said, "and filled his tank up there."

"Why would he?"

Dave smiled. It gave him a surprisingly foxy look that

was not much like his usual expression of earnest and slightly stupid honesty. It occurred to Stephanie now that the intellect behind that chubby, rather childish face was probably as lean and quick as Vince Teague's.

"Cogan might've paid Mr. Denver Flyboy to do it that way because he was afraid of leaving a paper trail," Dave said. "And Mr. Denver Flyboy would very likely have gone along with any reasonable request if he was being paid enough."

"As for the Colorado Kid," Vince resumed, "he's still got almost two hours to get to Tinnock, get a fish-and-chips basket at Jan's Wharfside, sit at a table eating it while he looks out at the water, and then catch the last ferry to Moose-Lookit Island." As he spoke, he slowly brought Stephanie's left and right forefingers together until they touched.

Stephanie watched, fascinated. "Could he do it?"

"Maybe, but it'd be awful goddamned tight," Dave said with a sigh. "*I'd* have never believed it if he hadn't actually turned up dead on Hammock Beach. Would you, Vince?"

"Nup," Vince said, without even pausing to consider.

Dave said, "There's four dirt airstrips within a dozen miles or so of Tinnock, all seasonal. They do most of their trade takin up tourists on sight-seein rides in the summer, or to look at the fall foliage when the colors peak out, although that only lasts a couple of weeks. We checked em on the off-chance that Cogan might have chartered him a second plane, this one a little prop-job like a Piper Cub, and flown from Bangor to the coast."

"No joy there, either, I take it."

"You take it right," Vince said, and his grin was gloomy rather than foxy. "Once those elevator doors slide closed on Cogan in that Denver office building, this whole business is nothing but shadows you can't quite catch hold of…and one dead body.

"Three of those four airstrips were deserted in April, shut right down, so a plane *could* have flown in to any of em and no one the wiser. The fourth one—a woman named Maisie Harrington lived out there with her father and about sixty mutt dogs, and she claimed that no one flew into their strip from October of 1979 to May of 1980, but she smelled like a distillery, and I had my doubts if she could remember what went on a *week* before I talked to her, let alone a year and a half before."

"What about the woman's father?" she asked.

"Stone blind and one-legged," Dave said. "The diabetes."

"Ouch," she said.

"Ayuh."

"Let Jack n Maisie Harrington go hang," Vince said impatiently. "I never believed in the Second Airplane Theory when it comes to Cogan any more than I ever believed in the Second Gunman Theory when it came to Kennedy. If Cogan had a car waiting for him in Denver—and I can't see any way around it—then he could have had one waiting for him at the General Aviation Terminal, as well. And I believe he did."

"That is just so far-fetched," Dave said. He spoke not scoffingly but dolefully.

"P'raps," Vince responded, unperturbed, "but when you get rid of the impossible, whatever's left…there's your pup, scratchin at the door t'be let in."

"He could have driven himself," Stephanie said thoughtfully.

"A rental car?" Dave shook his head. "Don't think so, dear. Rental agencies take only credit cards, and credit cards leave paper trails."

"Besides," Vince said, "Cogan didn't know his way around eastern and coastal Maine. So far as we can discover, he'd never been here in his life. You know the roads by now, Steffi: there's only one main one that comes out this way from Bangor to Ellsworth, but once you get to Ellsworth, there's three or four different choices, and a flatlander, even one with a map, is apt to get confused. No, I think Dave is right. If the Kid meant to go by car, and if he knew in advance how small his time-window was going to be, he would have wanted to have a driver standin by and waitin. Somebody who'd take cash money, drive fast, and not get lost."

Stephanie thought for a little while. The two old men let her.

"*Three* hired drivers in all," she said at last. "The one in the middle at the controls of a private jet."

"Maybe with a copilot," Dave put in quietly. "Them are the rules, at least."

"It's very outlandish," she said.

Vince nodded and sighed. "I don't disagree."

"You've never turned up even one of these drivers, have you?"

"No."

She thought some more, this time with her head down and her normally smooth brow furrowed in a deep frown. Once more they did not interrupt her, and after perhaps two minutes, she looked up again. "But *why*? What could be so important for Cogan to go to such lengths?"

Vince Teague and Dave Bowie looked at each other, then back at her. Vince said: "Ain't *that* a good question."

Dave said: "A *rig* of a question."

Vince said: "The *main* question."

"Accourse it is," Dave said. "Always was."

Vince, quite softly: "We don't know, Stephanie. We never have."

Dave, more softly still: "Boston *Globe* wouldn't like that. Nope, not at all."

# 17

"Accourse, we ain't the Boston *Globe*," Vince said. "We ain't even the Bangor *Daily News*. But Stephanie, when a grown man or woman goes completely off the rails, every newspaper writer, big town or small one, looks for certain reasons. It don't matter whether the result is most of the Methodist church picnic windin up poisoned or just the gentlemanly half of a marriage quietly disappearin one weekday morning, never to be seen alive again. Now—for the time bein never mindin where he wound up, or the improbability of how he managed to get there—tell me what some of those reasons for goin off the rails might be. Count them off for me until I see at least four of your fingers in the air."

*School is in session,* she thought, and then remembered something Vince had said to her a month before, almost in passing: *To be a success in the news business, it don't hurt to have a dirty mind, dear.* At the time she'd thought the remark bizarre, perhaps even borderline senile. Now she thought she understood a little better.

"Sex," she said, raising her left forefinger—her Colorado Kid finger. "I.e., another woman." She popped another finger. "Money problems, I'm thinking either debt or theft."

"Don't forget the IRS," Dave said. "People sometimes run when they realize they're in hock to Uncle Sam."

"She don't know how boogery the IRS can be," Vince said. "You can't hold that against her. Anyway, according to his wife Cogan had no problems with Infernal Revenue. Go on, Steffi, you're doin fine."

She didn't yet have enough fingers in the air to satisfy him, but could think of only one other thing. "The urge to start a brand-new life?" she asked doubtfully, seeming to speak more to herself than to them. "To just…I don't know …cut all the ties and start over again as a different person in a different place?" And then something else *did* occur to her. "Madness?" She had four fingers up now—one for sex, one for money, one for change, one for madness. She looked doubtfully at the last two. "Maybe change and madness are the same?"

"Maybe they are," Vince said. "And you could argue that madness covers all sorts of addictions that people try to run from. That sort of running's sometimes known as the 'geographic cure.' I'm thinking specifically of drugs and alcohol. Gambling's another addiction people try the geographic cure on, but I guess you could file that problem under money."

"Did he have drug or alcohol problems?"

"Arla Cogan said not, and I believe she would have known. And after sixteen months to think it over, and with him dead at the end of it, I think she would have told me."

"But, Steffi," Dave said (and rather gently), "when you consider it, madness almost *has* to be in it somewhere, wouldn't you say?"

She thought of James Cogan, the Colorado Kid, sitting dead on Hammock Beach with his back against a litter basket and a lump of meat lodged in his throat, his closed eyes turned in the direction of Tinnock and the reach beyond. She thought of how one hand had still been curled, as if holding the rest of his midnight snack, a piece of steak some hungry gull had no doubt stolen, leaving nothing but a sticky pattern of sand in the leftover grease on his palm. "Yes," she said. "There's madness in it somewhere. Did *she* know that? His wife?"

The two men looked at each other. Vince sighed and rubbed the side of his blade-thin nose. "She might have, but by then she had her own life to worry about, Steffi. Hers and her son's. A man up and disappears like that, the woman left behind is apt to have a damn hard skate. She got her old job back, working in one of the Boulder banks, but there was no way she could keep the house in Nederland—"

"Hernando's Hideaway," Stephanie murmured, feeling a sympathetic pang.

"Ayuh, that. She kept on her feet without having to borrow too much from her folks, or anything at all from his, but she used up most of the money they'd put aside for little Mike's college education in the process. When we saw her, I should judge she wanted two things, one practical and one what you'd call...spiritual?" He looked rather doubtfully at Dave, who shrugged and nodded as if to say that word would do.

Vince nodded himself and went on. "She wanted to be

shed of the not-knowing. Was he alive or dead? Was she married or a widow? Could she lay hope to rest or did she have to carry it yet awhile longer? Maybe that last sounds a trifle hard-hearted, and maybe it is, but I should think that after sixteen months, hope must get damned heavy on your back—damned heavy to tote around.

"As for the practical, that was simple. She just wanted the insurance company to pay off what they owed. I know that Arla Cogan isn't the only person in the history of the world to hate an insurance company, but I'd have to put her high on the list for sheer intensity. She'd been going along and going along, you see, her and Michael, living in a three- or four-room apartment in Boulder—quite a change after the nice house in Nederland—and her leaving him in daycare and with babysitters she wasn't always sure she could trust, working a job she didn't really want to do, going to bed alone after years of having someone to snuggle up to, worrying over the bills, always watching the needle on the gas-gauge because the price of gasoline was going up even then…and all the time she was sure in her heart that he was dead, but the insurance company wouldn't pay off because of what her heart knew, not when there was no body, let alone a cause of death.

"She kept asking me if 'the bastards'—that's what she always called em—could 'wiggle off' somehow, if they could claim it was suicide. I told her I'd never heard of someone committing suicide by choking themselves on a piece of meat, and later, after she had made the formal identification of the death-photo in Cathcart's presence, he told her the same thing. That seemed to ease her mind a little bit.

"Cathcart pitched right in, said he'd call the company agent in Brighton, Colorado, and explain about the fingerprints and her photo I.D. Nail everything down tight. She cried quite a little bit at that—some in relief, some in gratitude, some just from exhaustion, I guess."

"Of course," Stephanie murmured.

"I took her across to Moosie on the ferry and put her up at the Red Roof Motel," Vince continued. "Same place you stayed when you first got here, wasn't it?"

"Yes," Stephanie said. She had been at a boarding house for the last month or so, but would look for something more permanent in October. If, that was, these two old birds would keep her on. She thought they would. She thought that was, in large part, what this was all about.

"The three of us had breakfast the next morning," Dave said, "and like most people who haven't done anything wrong and haven't had much experience with newspapers, she had no shyness about talking to us. No sense that any of what she was sayin might later turn up on page one." He paused. "And accourse very little of it ever did. It was never the kind of story that sees much in the way of print, once you get past the main fact of the matter: Man Found Dead On Hammock Beach, Coroner Says No Foul Play. And by then, that was cold news, indeed."

"No through-line," Stephanie said.

"No *nothing*!" Dave cried, and then laughed until he coughed. When that cleared, he wiped the corners of his eyes with a large paisley handkerchief he pulled from the back pocket of his pants.

"What did she tell you?" Stephanie asked.

"What *could* she tell us?" Vince responded. "Mostly what she did was ask questions. The only one I asked her was if the *chervonetz* was a lucky piece or a memento or something like that." He snorted. "Some newspaperman I was that day."

"The *chevron*—" She gave up on it, shaking her head.

"The Russian coin in his pocket, mixed in with the rest of his change," Vince said. "It was a *chervonetz*. A ten-ruble piece. I asked her if he kept it as a lucky piece or something. She didn't have a clue. Said the closest Jim had ever been to Russia was when they rented a James Bond movie called *From Russia With Love* at Blockbuster."

"He might have picked it up on the beach," she said thoughtfully. "People find all sorts of things on the beach." She herself had found a woman's high-heel shoe, worn exotically smooth from many a long tumble between the sea and the shore, while walking one day on Little Hay Beach, about two miles from Hammock.

"Might've, ayuh," Vince agreed. He looked at her, his eyes twinkling in their deep sockets. "Want to know the two things I remember best about her the morning after her appointment with Cathcart over in Tinnock?"

"Sure."

"How *rested* she looked. And how well she ate when we sat down to breakfast."

"That's a fact," Dave agreed. "There's that old sayin

about how the condemned man ate a hearty meal, but I've got an idea that no one eats so hearty as the man—or the woman—who's finally been up and pardoned. And in a way she had been. She might not have known why he came to our part of the world, or what befell him once he got here, and I think she realized she might not ever know—"

"She did," Vince agreed. "She said so when I drove her back to the airport."

"—but she knew the only important thing: he was dead. Her heart might have been telling her that all along, but her head needed proof to go along for the ride."

"Not to mention in order to convince that pesky insurance company," Dave said.

"Did she ever get the money?" Stephanie asked.

Dave smiled. "Yes, ma'am. They dragged their feet some—those boys have a tendency to go fast when they're putting on the sell-job and then slow down when someone puts in a claim—but finally they paid. We got a letter to that effect, thanking us for all our hard work. She said that without us, she'd still be wondering and the insurance company would still be claiming that James Cogan could be alive in Brooklyn or Tangiers."

"What kind of questions did she ask?"

"The ones you'd expect," Vince said. "First thing she wanted to know was where he went when he got off the ferry. We couldn't tell her. We asked questions—didn't we, Dave?"

Dave Bowie nodded.

"But no one remembered seein him," Vince continued. "Accourse it would have been almost full dark by then, so there's no real reason why anyone should have. As for the few other passengers—and at that time of year there aren't many, especially on the last ferry of the day—they would have gone right to their cars in the Bay Street parkin lot, heads down in their collars because of the wind off the reach."

"And she asked about his wallet," Dave said. "All we could tell her was that no one ever found it...at least no one who ever turned it in to the police. I suppose it's possible someone could have picked it out of his pocket on the ferry, stripped the cash out of it, then dropped it overside."

"It's possible that heaven's a rodeo, too, but not likely," Vince said drily. "If he had cash in his wallet, why did he have more—seventeen dollars in paper money—in his pants pocket?"

"Just in case," Stephanie said.

"Maybe," Vince said, "but it doesn't feel right to me. And frankly, I find the idea of a pickpocket workin the six o'clock ferry between Tinnock and Moosie a touch more unbelievable than a commercial artist from a Denver advertising agency charterin a jet to fly to New England."

"In any case, we couldn't tell her where his wallet went," Dave said, "or where his topcoat and suit-jacket went, or why he was found sittin out there on a stretch of beach in nothin but his pants and shirt."

"The cigarettes?" Stephanie asked. "I bet she was curious about those."

Vince barked a laugh. "Curious isn't the right word. That pack of smokes drove her almost crazy. She couldn't understand why he'd have had cigarettes on him. And we didn't need her to tell us he wasn't the kind who'd stopped for awhile and then decided to take the habit up again. Cathcart took a good look at his lungs during the autopsy, for reasons I'm sure you'll understand—"

"He wanted to make sure he hadn't drowned after all?" Stephanie asked.

"That's right," Vince said. "If Dr. Cathcart had found water in the lungs beneath that chunk of meat, it would have suggested someone trying to cover up the way Mr. Cogan actually died. And while that wouldn't have proved murder, it would've suggested it. Cathcart *didn't* find water in Cogan's lungs, and he didn't find any evidence of smoking, either. Nice and pink down there, he said. Yet someplace between Cogan's office building and Stapleton Airport, and in spite of the tearing hurry he had to've been in, he must've had his driver stop so he could pick up a pack. Either that or he had em put by already, which is what I tend to believe. Maybe with his Russian coin."

"Did you tell her that?" Stephanie asked.

"No," Vince said, and just then the telephone rang. "'Scuse me," he said, and went to answer it.

He spoke briefly, said *Ayuh* a time or three, then returned, stretching his back some more as he did. "That was Ellen Dunwoodie," he said. "She's ready to talk about the great trauma she's been through, snappin off that fire hydrant and 'makin a spectacle of herself.' That's an exact quote, although I don't think it will appear in my pulse-poundin account of the event. In any case, I think I'd better amble over there pretty soon; get the story while her recollection's clear and before she decides to make supper. I'm lucky she n her sister eat late. Otherwise I'd be out of luck."

"And I've *got* to get after those invoices," Dave said. "Seems like there must be a dozen more than there were when we left for the Gull. I swan to goodness when you leave em alone atop a desk, they breed."

Stephanie gazed at them with real alarm. "You can't stop now. You can't just leave me hanging."

"No other choice," Vince said mildly. "*We've* been hanging, Steffi, and for twenty-five years now. There isn't any jilted church secretary in this one."

"No Ellsworth city lights reflected on the clouds down-east, either," Dave said. "Not even a Teodore Riponeaux in the picture, some poor old sailorman murdered for hypo-thetical pirate treasure and then left dead on the foredeck after all his shipmates had been tossed overside—and why? As a warning to other would-be treasure-hunters, by gorry! Now *there's* a through-line for you, dearheart!"

Dave grinned…but then the grin faded. "Nothing like that in the case of the Colorado Kid; no string for the beads, don't you see, and no Sherlock Holmes or Ellery Queen to string em in any case. Just a couple of guys running a news-paper with about a hundred stories a week to cover. None of em drawin much water by Boston *Globe* standards, but stuff people on the island like to read about, all the same. Speakin of which, weren't you going to talk with Sam Gernerd? Find out all the details on his famous Hayride, Dance, and Picnic?"

"I was…I am…and I *want* to! Do you guys understand

that? That I actually *want* to talk to him about that dumb thing?"

Vince Teague burst out laughing, and Dave joined him.

"Ayuh," Vince said, when he could talk again. "Dunno what the head of your journalism department would make of it, Steffi, he'd probably break down n cry, but I know you do." He glanced at Dave. "*We* know you do."

"And I know you've got your own fish to fry, but you must have *some* ideas…some *theories*…after all these years…" She looked at them plaintively. "I mean…don't you?"

They glanced at each other and again she felt that telepathy flow between them, but this time she had no sense of the thought it carried. Then Dave looked back at her. "What is it you really want to know, Stephanie? Tell us."

# 18

"Do you think he was murdered?" *That* was what she really wanted to know. They had asked her to set the idea aside, and she had, but now the discussion of the Colorado Kid was almost over, and she thought they would allow her to put the subject back on the table.

"Why would you think that any more likely than accidental death, given everything we've told you?" Dave asked. He sounded genuinely curious.

"Because of the cigarettes. The cigarettes almost had to have been deliberate on his part. He just never thought it would take a year and a half for someone to discover that Colorado stamp. Cogan believed a man found dead on a beach with no identification would rate more investigation than he got."

"*Yes,*" Vince said. He spoke in a low voice but actually clenched a fist and shook it, like a fan who has just watched a ballplayer make a key play or deliver a clutch hit. "Good girl. Good job."

Although just twenty-two, there were people Stephanie would have resented for calling her a girl. This ninety-year-old man with the thin white hair, narrow face, and piercing blue eyes was not one of them. In truth, she flushed with pleasure.

"He couldn't know he'd draw a couple of thuds like O'Shanny and Morrison when it came time to investigate his death," Dave said. "Couldn't know he'd have to depend on a grad student who'd spent the last couple of months holdin briefcases and goin out for coffee, not to mention a couple of old guys puttin out a weekly paper one step above a supermarket handout."

"Hang on there, brother," Vince said. "Them's fightin words." He put up his elderly dukes, but with a grin.

"I think he did all right," Stephanie said. "In the end, I think he did just fine." And then, thinking of the woman and baby Michael (who would by this time be in his mid-twenties): "So did she, actually. Without Paul Devane and you two guys, Arla Cogan never would have gotten her insurance money."

"Some truth to that," Vince conceded. She was amused to see that something in this made him uncomfortable. Not that he'd done good, she thought, but that someone *knew* he had done good. They had the Internet out here; you could see a little Direct TV satellite dish on just about every house; no fishing boat set to sea anymore without the GPS switched on. Yet still the old Calvinist ideas ran deep. *Let not thy left hand know what thy right hand doeth.*

"What exactly do you think happened?" she asked.

"No, Steffi," Vince said. He spoke kindly but firmly. "You're still expectin Rex Stout to come waltzin out of the closet, or Ellery Queen arm in arm with Miss Jane Marple. If we knew what happened, if we had any idea, we would have chased that idea til we dropped. And frig the Boston *Globe*, we would have broken any story we found on page one of the *Islander*. We may have been *little* newspapermen back in '81, and we may be little *old* newspapermen now, but we ain't *dead* little old newspapermen. I still like the idea of a big story just fine."

"Me too," Dave said. He'd gotten up, probably with those invoices on his mind, but had now settled on the corner of his desk, swinging one large leg. "I've always dreamed of us havin a story that got syndicated nationwide, and that's one dream I'll probably die with. Go on, Vince, tell her as much as you think. She'll keep it close. She's one of us now."

Stephanie almost shivered with pleasure, but Vince Teague appeared not to notice. He leaned forward, fixing her light blue eyes with his, which were a much darker shade—the color of the ocean on a sunny day.

"All right," he said. "I started to think something might be funny about how he died as well as how he got here long before all that about the stamp. I started askin myself questions when I realized he had a pack of cigarettes with only one gone, although he'd been on the island since at least six-thirty. I made a real pest of myself at Bayside News."

Vince smiled at the recollection.

"I showed everyone at the shop Cogan's picture, including the sweep-up boy. I was convinced he must have bought that pack there, unless he got it out of a vendin machine at a place like the Red Roof or the Shuffle Inn or maybe Sonny's Sunoco. The way I figured, he must have finished his smokes while wanderin around Moosie, after gettin off the ferry, then bought a fresh supply. And I *also* figured that if he got em at the News, he must have gotten em shortly before eleven, which is when the News closes. That would explain why he just smoked one, and only used one of his new matches, before he died."

"But then you found out he wasn't a smoker at all," Stephanie said.

"That's right. His wife said so and Cathcart confirmed it. And later on I became sure that pack of smokes was a message: *I came from Colorado, look for me there*."

"We'll never know for sure, but we both think that's what it was," Dave said.

"Jee-*sus*," she almost whispered. "So where does that lead you?"

Once more they looked at each other and shrugged those identical shrugs. "Into a land of shadows n moonbeams," Vince said. "Places no feature writer from the Boston *Globe* will ever go, in other words. But there are a few things I'm sure of in my heart. Would you like to hear em?"

"Yes!"

Vince spoke slowly but deliberately, like a man feeling his way down a very dark corridor where he has been many times before.

"He knew he was goin into a desperate situation, and he knew he might go unidentified if he died. He didn't want that to happen, quite likely because he was worried about leaving his wife broke."

"So he bought those cigarettes, hoping they'd be over-looked," Stephanie said.

Vince nodded. "Ayuh, and they were."

"But overlooked by *who*?"

Vince paused, then went on without answering her question. "He went down in the elevator and out through the lobby of his building. There was a car waitin to take him to Stapleton Airport, either right there or just around the corner. Maybe it was just him and the driver in that car; maybe there was someone else. We'll never know. You asked me earlier if Cogan was wearing his overcoat when he left that morning, and I said George the Artist didn't remember, but Arla said she never saw that overcoat no more, so maybe he was, at that. If so, I think he took it off in the car or in the airplane. I think he also took off his suit-coat jacket. I think someone either gave him the green jacket to wear in their place, or it was waitin for him."

"In the car or on the plane."

"Ayuh," Dave said.

"The cigarettes?"

"Don't know for sure, but if I had to bet, I'd bet he already had em on him," Dave said. "He knew this was comin along...whatever *this* was. He'd've had em in his pants pocket, I think."

"Then, later, on the beach..." She saw Cogan, her mind's-eye version of the Colorado Kid, lighting his life's first cigarette—first and last—and then strolling down to the water's edge with it, there on Hammock Beach, alone in the moonlight. The midnight moonlight. He takes one puff of the harsh, unfamiliar smoke. Maybe two. Then he throws the cigarette into the sea. Then...what?

*What?*

"The plane dropped him off in Bangor," she heard herself saying in a voice that sounded harsh and unfamiliar to her.

"Ayuh," Dave agreed.

"And his ride from Bangor dropped him off in Tinnock."

"Ayuh." That was Vince.

"He ate a fish-and-chips basket."

"So he did," Vince agreed. "Autopsy proves it. So did my nose. I smelled the vinegar."

"Was his wallet gone by then?"

"We don't know," Dave said. "We'll never know. But I think so. I think he gave it up with his topcoat, his suit-coat, and his normal life. I think what he got in return was a green jacket, which he also gave up later on."

"Or had taken from his dead body," Vince said.

Stephanie shivered. She couldn't help it. "He rides across to Moose-Lookit Island on the six o'clock ferry, bringing Gard Edwick a paper cup of coffee on the way—what could be construed as tea for the tillerman, or the ferryman."

"Yuh," Dave said. He looked very solemn.

"By then he has no wallet, no ID, just seventeen dollars and some change that maybe includes a Russian ten-ruble coin. Do you think that coin might have been…oh, I don't know…some sort of identification-thingy, like in a spy novel? I mean, the cold war between Russia and the United States would have still been going on then, right?"

"Full blast," Vince said. "But Steffi—if you were going to dicker with a Russian secret agent, would you use a *ruble* to introduce yourself?"

"No," she admitted. "But why else would he have it? To show it to someone, that's all I can think of."

"I've always had the intuition that someone gave it to *him*," Dave said. "Maybe along with a piece of cold sirloin steak, wrapped up in a piece of tinfoil."

"Why?" she asked. "Why would they?"

Dave shook his head. "I don't know."

"Was there tinfoil found at the scene? Maybe thrown into that sea-grass along the far edge of the beach?"

"O'Shanny and Morrison sure didn't look," Dave said. "Me n Vince had a hunt all around Hammock Beach after that yella tape was taken down—not specifically for tinfoil, you understand, but for anything that looked like it might bear on the dead man, anything at all. We found nothing but the usual litter—candy-wrappers and such."

"If the meat was in foil or a Baggie, the Kid might very well have tossed it into the water, along with his one cigarette," Vince said.

"About that piece of meat in his throat…"

Vince was smiling a little. "I had several long conversations about that piece of steak with both Doc Robinson and Dr. Cathcart. Dave was in on a couple of em. I remember Cathcart saying to me once, this had to've been not more than a month before the heart attack that took his life six or seven years ago, 'You go back to that old business the way a kid who's lost a tooth goes back to the hole with the tip of his tongue.' And I thought to myself, yep, that's exactly right, exactly what it's like. It's like a hole I can't stop poking at and licking into, trying to find the bottom of.

"First thing I wanted to know was if that piece of meat could have been jammed down Cogan's throat, either with fingers or some sort of instrument like a lobster-pick, after he was dead. And that's crossed *your* mind, hasn't it?"

Stephanie nodded.

"He said it was possible but unlikely, because that piece of steak had not only been chewed, but chewed enough to be swallowed. It wasn't really meat at all anymore, but rather what Cathcart called 'organic pulp-mass.' Someone else could have chewed it that much, but would have been unlikely to have planted it after doing so, for fear it would have looked insufficient to cause death. Are you with me?"

She nodded again.

"He *also* said that meat chewed to a pulp-mass would be hard to manipulate with an instrument. It would tend to break up when pushed from the back of the mouth into the throat. Fingers could do it, but Cathcart said he believed he would have seen signs of that, most likely straining of the jaw ligatures." He paused, thinking, then shook his head. "There's a technical term for that kind of jaw-poppin, but I don't remember it."

"Tell her what Robinson told you," Dave said. His eyes were sparkling. "It didn't come to nummore'n the rest in the end, but I always thought it was *wicked* int'restin.'"

"He said there were certain muscle relaxants, some of em exotic, and Cogan's midnight snack might have been treated with one of those," Vince said. "He might get the first few bites down all right, accounting for what was found in his stomach, and then find himself all at once with a bite he wasn't able to swallow once it was chewed."

"That must have been it!" Stephanie cried. "Whoever dosed the meat sat there and just watched him choke! Then, when Cogan was dead, the murderer propped him up against the litter basket and took away the rest of the steak so it could never be tested! It was never a gull at all! It…" She stopped, looking at them. "Why are you shaking your heads?"

"The autopsy, dear," Vince said. "Nothing like that showed up on the blood-gas chromatograph tests."

"But if it was something exotic enough…"

"Like in an Agatha Christie yarn?" Vince asked, with a wink and a little smile. "Well, maybe…but there was also the piece of meat in his throat, don't you know."

"Oh. Right. Dr. Cathcart had that to test, didn't he?" She slumped a little.

"Ayuh," Vince agreed, "and did. We may be country mice, but we *do* have the occasional dark thought. And the closest thing to poison on that chunk of chewed-up meat was a little salt."

She was silent for a moment. Then she said (in a very low voice): "Maybe it was the kind of stuff that disappears."

"Ayuh," Dave said, and his tongue rounded the inside of one cheek. "Like the Coast Lights after an hour or two."

"Or the rest of the *Lisa Cabot*'s crew," Vince added.

"And once he got off the ferry, you don't know where he went."

"No, ma'am," Vince said. "We've looked off n on for over twenty-five years and never found a soul who claims to have seen him before Johnny and Nancy did around quarter past six on the morning of April 24th. And for the record—not that anyone's keepin one—I don't believe that anyone took what remained of that steak from his hand after he choked on his last bite. I believe a seagull stole the last of it from his dead hand, just as we always surmised. And gorry, I really *do* have to get a move on."

"And I have to get with those invoices," Dave said. "But first, I think another little rest-stop might be in order." That said, he lumbered toward the bathroom.

"I suppose I better get with this column," Stephanie said. Then she burst out, half-laughing and half-serious: "But I almost wish you hadn't told me, if you were going to leave me hanging! It'll be *weeks* before I get this out of my mind!"

"It's been twenty-five years, and it's still not out of ours," Vince said. "And at least you know why we didn't tell that guy from the *Globe*."

"Yes. I do."

He smiled and nodded. "You'll do all right, Stephanie. You'll do fine." He gave her shoulder a friendly squeeze, then started for the door, grabbing his narrow reporter's notebook from his littered desk on his way by and stuffing it into his back pocket. He was ninety but still walked easy, his back only slightly bent with age. He wore a gentleman's white shirt, its back crisscrossed with a gentleman's suspenders. Halfway across the room he stopped and turned to her again. A shaft of late sunlight caught his baby-fine white hair and turned it into a halo.

"You've been a pleasure to have around," he said. "I want you to know that."

"Thank you." She hoped she didn't sound as close to

tears as she suddenly felt. "It's been wonderful. I was a little dubious at first, but…but now I guess it goes right back at you. It's a pleasure to be here."

"Have you thought about staying? I think you have."

"Yes. You bet I have."

He nodded gravely. "Dave and I have spoken about that. It'd be good to have some new blood on the staff. Some young blood."

"You guys'll go on for years," she said.

"Oh yes," he said, off-handedly, as if that were a given, and when he died six months later, Stephanie would sit in a cold church, taking notes on the service in her own narrow reporter's book, and think: *He knew it was coming*. "I'll be around for years yet. Still, if you wanted to stay, we'd like to have you. You don't have to answer one way or another now, but consider it an offer."

"All right, I will. And I think we both know what the answer will be."

"That's fine, then." He started to turn, then turned back one last time. "School's almost out for the day, but I could tell you one more thing about our business. May I?"

"Of course."

"There are thousands of papers and *tens* of thousands of people writing stories for em, but there are only two types of stories. There are news stories, which usually aren't stories at all, but only accounts of unfolding events. Things like that don't *have* to be stories. People pick up a newspaper to read about the blood and the tears the way they slow down to look at a wreck on the highway, and then they move on. But what do they find inside of their newspaper?"

"Feature stories," Stephanie said, thinking of Hanratty and his unexplained mysteries.

"Ayuh. And those *are* stories. Every one of em has a beginning, a middle, and an end. That makes em happy news, Steffi, always happy news. Even if the story is about a church secretary who probably killed half the congregation at the church picnic because her lover jilted her, that is happy news, and why?"

"I don't know."

"You better," Dave said, emerging from the bathroom and still wiping his hands on a paper towel. "You better know if you want to be in this business, and understand what it is you're doin." He cast the paper towel into his wastebasket on his way by.

She thought about it. "Feature stories are happy stories because they're over."

"That's right!" Vince cried, beaming. He threw his hands in the air like a revival preacher. "They have *resolution*! They have *closure*! But do things have a beginning, a middle, and an end in real life, Stephanie? What does your experience tell you?"

"When it comes to newspaper work, I don't have much," she said. "Just the campus paper and, you know, Arts 'N Things here."

Vince waved this away. "Your heart n mind, what do they tell you?"

"That life usually doesn't work that way." She was thinking of a certain young man who would have to be dealt with if she decided to stay here beyond her four months…and that dealing might be messy. Probably *would* be messy.

Rick would not take the news well, because in Rick's mind, that wasn't how the story was supposed to go.

"I never read a feature story that wasn't a lie," Vince said mildly, "but usually you can make a lie fit on the page. This one would never fit. Unless…" He gave a little shrug.

For a moment she didn't know what that shrug meant. Then she remembered something Dave had said not long after they'd gone out to sit on the deck to sit in the late August sunshine. *It's ours,* he'd said, sounding almost angry. *A guy from the* Globe, *a guy from away—he'd only muck it up.*

"If you'd given this to Hanratty, he *would've* used it, wouldn't he?" she asked them.

"Wasn't ours to give, because we don't own it," Vince said. "It belongs to whoever tracks it down."

Smiling a little, Stephanie shook her head. "I think that's disingenuous. I think you and Dave are the last two people alive who know the whole thing."

"We were," Dave said. "Now there's you, Steffi."

She nodded to him, acknowledging the implicit compliment, then turned her attention back to Vince Teague, eyebrows raised. After a second or two, he chuckled.

"We didn't tell him about the Colorado Kid because he would have taken a true unexplained mystery and made it into just another feature story," Vince said. "Not by changin any of the facts, but by emphasizing one thing—the concept of muscle-relaxants making it hard or impossible to swallow, let's say—and leavin something else out."

"That there was absolutely no sign of anything like that in this case, for instance," Stephanie said.

"Ayuh, maybe that, maybe something else. And maybe he would have written it that way on his own, simply because making a story out of things that ain't quite a story on their own gets to be a habit after a certain number of years in this business, or maybe his editor would have sent it back to him to do on a rewrite."

"Or the editor might've done it himself, if time was tight," Dave put in.

"Yep, editors have been known to do that, as well," Vince agreed. "In any case, the Colorado Kid would most likely have ended up bein installment number seven or eight in Hanratty's Unexplained Mysteries of New England series, something for people to marvel over for fifteen minutes or so on Sunday and line their kitty-litter boxes with on Monday."

"And it wouldn't be yours anymore," Stephanie said.

Dave nodded, but Vince waved his hand as if to say *Oh, pish-tush*. "That I could put up with, but it would've hung a lie around the neck of a man who ain't alive to refute it, and that I *won't* put up with. Because I don't have to." He glanced at his watch. "In any case, I'm on my horse. Whichever one of you's last out the door, be sure to lock it behind you, all right?"

Vince left. They watched him go, then Dave turned back to her. "Any more questions?"

She laughed. "A hundred, but none you or Vince could answer, I guess."

"Just as long as you don't get tired of askin em, that's fine." He wandered off to his desk, sat down, and pulled a stack of papers toward him with a sigh. Stephanie started back toward her own desk, then something caught her eye on the wall-length bulletin board at the far end of the room, opposite Vince's cluttered desk. She walked over for a closer look.

The left half of the bulletin board was layered with old front pages of the *Islander*, most yellowed and curling. High in the corner, all by itself, was the front page from the week of July 9th, 1952. The headline read **MYSTERY LIGHTS OVER HANCOCK FASCINATE THOUSANDS**. Below was a photograph credited to one Vincent Teague— who would have been just thirty-seven back then, if she had her math right. The crisp black-and-white showed a Little League field with a billboard in deep center reading **HANCOCK LUMBER ALWAYS KNOWS THE SCORE!** To Stephanie the photo looked as if it had been snapped at twilight. The few adults in the single set of sagging bleachers were standing and looking up into the sky. So was the ump, who stood straddling home plate with his mask in his right hand. One set of players—the visiting team, she assumed— was bunched tightly together around third base, as if for comfort. The other kids, wearing jeans and jerseys with the words **HANCOCK LUMBER** printed on the back, stood in a rough line across the infield, all staring upward. And on the mound the little boy who had been pitching held his glove up to one of the bright circles which hung in the sky just below the clouds, as if to touch that mystery, and bring it close, and open its heart, and know its story.

# Afterword

Depending on whether you liked or hated *The Colorado Kid* (I think for many people there'll be no middle ground on this one, and that's fine with me), you have my friend Scott to thank or blame. He brought me the news clipping that got it going.

Every writer of fiction has had somebody bring him or her a clipping from time to time, sure that the subject will make a wonderful story. "You'll only have to change it around a little," the clipping-bearer says with an optimistic smile. I don't know how this works with other writers, but it had never worked with me, and when Scott handed me an envelope with a cutting from a Maine newspaper inside, I expected more of the same. But my mother raised no ingrates, so I thanked him, took it home, and tossed it on my desk. A day or two later I tore the envelope open, read the feature story inside, and was immediately galvanized.

I have lost the clipping since, and for once Google, that twenty-first century idiot savant, has been of no help, so all I can do is summarize from memory, a notoriously unreliable reference source. Yet in this case that hardly matters, since the feature story was only the spark that lit

the little fire that burns through these pages, and not the
fire itself.

What caught my eye immediately upon unfolding the
clipping was a drawing of a bright red purse. The story
was of the young woman who had owned it. She was seen
one day walking the main street of a small island community off the coast of Maine with that red purse over her
arm. The next day she was found dead on one of the
island beaches, *sans* purse or identification of any kind.
Even the cause of her death was a mystery, and although
it was eventually put down to drowning, with alcohol perhaps a contributing factor, that diagnosis remains tentative
to this day.

The young woman was eventually identified, but not until
her remains had spent a long, lonely time in a mainland
crypt. And I was left again with a smack of that mystery the
Maine islands like Cranberry and Monhegan have always
held for me—their contrasting yet oddly complimentary
atmospheres of community and solitariness. There are few
places in America where the line between the little world
Inside and all the great world Outside is so firmly and deeply
drawn. Islanders are full of warmth for those who belong,
but they keep their secrets well from those who do not.
And—as Agatha Christie shows so memorably in *Ten Little
Indians*—there is no locked room so grand as an island,
even one where the mainland looks just a long step away
on a clear summer afternoon; no place so perfectly made
for a mystery.

Mystery is my subject here, and I am aware that many

readers will feel cheated, even angry, by my failure to provide a solution to the one posed. Is it because I had no solution to give? The answer is no. Should I have set my wits to work (as Richard Adams puts it in his forenote to *Shardik*), I could likely have provided half a dozen, three good, two a-country fair, and one fine as paint. I suspect many of you who have read the case know what some or all of them are. But in this one case—this very *hard* case, if I may be allowed a small pun on the imprint under whose cover the tale lies—I'm really not interested in the solution but in the mystery. Because it was the mystery that kept bringing me back to the story, day after day.

Did I care about those two old geezers, gnawing ceaselessly away at the case in their spare time even as the years went by and they grew ever more geezerly? Yes, I did. Did I care about Stephanie, who's clearly undergoing a kind of test, and being judged by kind but hard judges? Yes—I wanted her to pass. Was I happy with each little discovery, each small ray of light shed? Of course. But mostly what drew me on was the thought of the Colorado Kid, propped there against that trash barrel and looking out at the ocean, an anomaly that stretched even the most flexible credulity to the absolute snapping point. Maybe even a little beyond. In the end, I didn't care how he got there; like a nightingale glimpsed in the desert, it just took my breath away that he *was*.

And, of course, I wanted to see how my characters coped with the fact of him. It turned out they did quite well. I was proud of them. Now I will wait for my mail, both e- and of the snail variety, and see how *you* guys do with him.

I don't want to belabor the point, but before I leave you, I ask you to consider the fact that we live in a *web* of mystery, and have simply gotten so used to the fact that we have crossed out the word and replaced it with one we like better, that one being *reality*. Where do we come from? Where were we before we were here? Don't know. Where are we going? Don't know. A lot of churches have what they assure us are the answers, but most of us have a sneaking suspicion all that might be a con-job laid down to fill the collection plates. In the meantime, we're in a kind of compulsory dodgeball game as we free-fall from Wherever to Ain't Got A Clue. Sometimes bombs go off and sometimes the planes land okay and sometimes the blood tests come back clean and sometimes the biopsies come back positive. Most times the bad telephone call doesn't come in the middle of the night but sometimes it does, and either way we know we're going to drive pedal-to-the-metal into the mystery eventually.

It's crazy to be able to live with that and stay sane, but it's also beautiful. I write to find out what I think, and what I found out writing *The Colorado Kid* was that maybe—I just say *maybe*—it's the beauty of the mystery that allows us to live sane as we pilot our fragile bodies through this demolition-derby world. We always want to reach for the lights in the sky, and we always want to know where the Colorado Kid (the world is full of Colorado Kids) came from. Wanting might be better than knowing. I don't say that for sure; I only suggest it. But if you tell me I fell down on the job and didn't tell all of this story there was to tell, I say you're all wrong.

On that I *am* sure.

*Stephen King*
*January 31, 2005*

# If You Enjoyed
# THE COLORADO KID

## You'll Love
# JOYLAND

College student Devin Jones took the summer job at Joyland hoping to forget the girl who broke his heart. But he wound up facing something far more terrible: the legacy of a vicious murder, the fate of a dying child, and dark truths about life—and what comes after—that would change his world forever.

A riveting story about love and loss, about growing up and growing old—and about those who don't get to do either because death comes for them before their time—JOYLAND is Stephen King at the peak of his storytelling powers. With all the emotional impact of King masterpieces such as *The Green Mile* and *The Shawshank Redemption*, JOYLAND is at once a mystery, a horror story, and a bittersweet coming-of-age novel, one that will leave even the most hard-boiled reader profoundly moved.

*"Immensely appealing."*
— Washington Post

*"Tight and engrossing...a prize
worth all your tokens and skeeball tickets."*
— USA Today

**Read on for a preview—
or get a copy today
from your favorite
local or online bookseller!**

♥

I had a car, but on most days in that fall of 1973 I walked to
Joyland from Mrs. Shoplaw's Beachside Accommodations
in the town of Heaven's Bay. It seemed like the right thing
to do. The only thing, actually. By early September, Heaven
Beach was almost completely deserted, which suited my
mood. That fall was the most beautiful of my life. Even
forty years later I can say that. And I was never so unhappy,
I can say that, too. People think first love is sweet, and
never sweeter than when that first bond snaps. You've
heard a thousand pop and country songs that prove the
point; some fool got his heart broke. Yet that first broken
heart is always the most painful, the slowest to mend, and
leaves the most visible scar. What's so sweet about that?

♥

Through September and right into October, the North
Carolina skies were clear and the air was warm even at seven
in the morning, when I left my second-floor apartment by

the outside stairs. If I started with a light jacket on, I was wearing it tied around my waist before I'd finished half of the three miles between the town and the amusement park.

I'd make Betty's Bakery my first stop, grabbing a couple of still-warm croissants. My shadow would walk with me on the sand, at least twenty feet long. Hopeful gulls, smelling the croissants in their waxed paper, would circle overhead. And when I walked back, usually around five (although sometimes I stayed later—there was nothing waiting for me in Heaven's Bay, a town that mostly went sleepybye when summer was over), my shadow walked with me on the water. If the tide was in, it would waver on the surface, seeming to do a slow hula.

Although I can't be completely sure, I think the boy and the woman and their dog were there from the first time I took that walk. The shore between the town and the cheerful, blinking gimcrackery of Joyland was lined with summer homes, many of them expensive, most of them clapped shut after Labor Day. But not the biggest of them, the one that looked like a green wooden castle. A board-walk led from its wide back patio down to where the seagrass gave way to fine white sand. At the end of the boardwalk was a picnic table shaded by a bright green beach umbrella. In its shade, the boy sat in his wheelchair, wearing a baseball cap and covered from the waist down by a blanket even in the late afternoons, when the tempera-ture lingered in the seventies. I thought he was five or so, surely no older than seven. The dog, a Jack Russell terrier, either lay beside him or sat at his feet. The woman sat on one of the picnic table benches, sometimes reading a book, mostly just staring out at the water. She was very beautiful.

Going or coming, I always waved to them, and the boy waved back. She didn't, not at first. 1973 was the year of the OPEC oil embargo, the year Richard Nixon announced he was not a crook, the year Edward G. Robinson and Noel Coward died. It was Devin Jones's lost year. I was a twenty-one year-old virgin with literary aspirations. I possessed three pairs of bluejeans, four pairs of Jockey shorts, a clunker Ford (with a good radio), occasional suicidal ideations, and a broken heart.

Sweet, huh?

♥

The heartbreaker was Wendy Keegan, and she didn't deserve me. It's taken me most of my life to come to that conclusion, but you know the old saw; better late than never. She was from Portsmouth, New Hampshire; I was from South Berwick, Maine. That made her practically the girl next door. We had begun "going together" (as we used to say) during our freshman year at UNH—we actually met at the Freshman Mixer, and how sweet is that? Just like one of those pop songs.

We were inseparable for two years, went everywhere together and did everything together. Everything, that is, but "it." We were both work-study kids with University jobs. Hers was in the library; mine was in the Commons cafeteria. We were offered the chance to hold onto those jobs during the summer of 1972, and of course we did. The money wasn't great, but the togetherness was priceless. I assumed that would also be the deal during the summer of 1973, until Wendy announced that her friend Renee had gotten them jobs working at Filene's, in Boston.

"Where does that leave me?" I asked.

"You can always come down," she said. "I'll miss you like mad, but really, Dev, we could probably use some time apart."

A phrase that is very often a death-knell. She may have seen that idea on my face, because she stood on tiptoe and kissed me. "Absence makes the heart grow fonder," she said. "Besides, with my own place, maybe you can stay over." But she didn't quite look at me when she said that, and I never did stay over. Too many roommates, she said. Too little time. Of course such problems can be overcome, but somehow we never did, which should have told me something; in retrospect, it tells me a lot. Several times we had been very close to "it," but "it" just never quite happened. She always drew back, and I never pressed her. God help me, I was being gallant. I have wondered often since what would have changed (for good or for ill) had I not been. What I know now is that gallant young men rarely get pussy. Put it on a sampler and hang it in your kitchen.

♥

The prospect of another summer mopping cafeteria floors and loading elderly Commons dishwashers with dirty plates didn't hold much charm for me, not with Wendy seventy miles south, enjoying the bright lights of Boston, but it was steady work, which I needed, and I didn't have any other prospects. Then, in late February, one literally came down the dish-line to me on the conveyor belt.

Someone had been reading *Carolina Living* while he or she snarfed up that day's blue plate luncheon special, which happened to be Mexicali Burgers and Caramba Fries. He or she had left the magazine on the tray, and I picked it up along with the dishes. I almost tossed it in the trash, then didn't. Free reading material was, after all, free reading material. (I was a work-study kid, remember.) I stuck it in my back pocket and forgot about it until I got back to my dorm room. There it flopped onto the floor, open to the classified section at the back, while I was changing my pants.

Whoever had been reading the magazine had circled several job possibilities...although in the end, he or she must have decided none of them was quite right; otherwise *Carolina Living* wouldn't have come riding down the conveyor belt. Near the bottom of the page was an ad that caught my eye even though it hadn't been circled. In bold-face type, the first line read: WORK CLOSE TO HEAVEN! What English major could read that and not hang in for the pitch? And what glum twenty-one-year-old, beset with the growing fear that he might be losing his girlfriend, would not be attracted by the idea of working in a place called Joyland?

There was a telephone number, and on a whim, I called it. A week later, a job application landed in my dormitory mailbox. The attached letter stated that if I wanted full-time summer employment (which I did), I'd be doing many different jobs, most but not all custodial. I would have to possess a valid driver's license, and I would need to interview. I could do that on the upcoming spring break instead of going home to Maine for the week. Only I'd been planning to spend at least some of that week with Wendy. We might even get around to "it."

"Go for the interview," Wendy said when I told her. She didn't even hesitate. "It'll be an adventure."

"Being with you would be an adventure," I said.

"There'll be plenty of time for that next year." She stood on tiptoe and kissed me (she always stood on tiptoe). Was she seeing the other guy, even then? Probably not, but I'll bet she'd noticed him, because he was in her Advanced Sociology course. Renee St. Claire would have known, and probably would have told me if I'd asked—telling stuff was Renee's specialty, I bet she wore the priest out when she did the old confession bit—but some things you don't want to know. Like why the girl you loved with all your heart kept saying no to you, but tumbled into bed with the new guy at almost the first opportunity. I'm not sure anybody ever gets completely over their first love, and that still rankles. Part of me still wants to know what was *wrong* with me. What I was lacking. I'm in my sixties now, my hair is gray and I'm a prostate cancer survivor, but I still want to know why I wasn't good enough for Wendy Keegan.

♥

I took a train called the Southerner from Boston to North Carolina (not much of an adventure, but cheap), and a bus from Wilmington to Heaven's Bay. My interview was with Fred Dean, who was—among many other functions—Joyland's employment officer. After fifteen minutes of Q-and-A, plus a look at my driver's license and my Red Cross life-saving certificate, he handed me a plastic badge on a lanyard. It bore the word VISITOR, that day's date, and a cartoon picture of a grinning, blue-eyed German Shepherd who bore a passing resemblance to the famous cartoon sleuth, Scooby-Doo.

"Take a walk around," Dean said. "Ride the Carolina Spin, if you like. Most of the rides aren't up and running yet, but that one is. Tell Lane I said okay. What I gave you is a day-pass, but I want you back here by…" He looked at his watch. "Let's say one o'clock. Tell me then if you want the job. I've got five spots left, but they're all basically the same—as Happy Helpers."

"Thank you, sir."

He nodded, smiling. "Don't know how you'll feel about this place, but it suits me fine. It's a little old and a little rickety, but I find that charming. I tried Disney for a while; didn't like it. It's too…I don't know…"

"Too corporate?" I ventured.

"Exactly. Too corporate. Too buffed and shiny. So I came back to Joyland a few years ago. Haven't regretted it. We fly a bit more by the seat of our pants here—the place has a little of the old-time carny flavor. Go on, look around. See what you think. More important, see how you *feel*."

"Can I ask one question first?"

"Of course."

I fingered my day pass. "Who's the dog?"

His smile became a grin. "That's Howie the Happy Hound, Joyland's mascot. Bradley Easterbrook built Joyland, and the original Howie was his dog. Long dead now, but you'll still see a lot of him, if you work here this summer."

I did…and I didn't. An easy riddle, but the explanation will have to wait awhile.

♥

Joyland was an indie, not as big as a Six Flags park, and nowhere near as big as Disney World, but it was large enough to be impressive, especially with Joyland Avenue, the main drag, and Hound Dog Way, the secondary drag, almost empty and looking eight lanes wide. I heard the whine of power-saws and saw plenty of workmen—the largest crew swarming over the Thunderball, one of Joyland's two coasters—but there were no customers, because the park didn't open until June fifteenth. A few of the food concessions were doing business to take care of the workers' lunch needs, though, and an old lady in front of a star-studded tell-your-fortune kiosk was staring at me suspiciously. With one exception, everything else was shut up tight.

The exception of the Carolina Spin. It was a hundred and seventy feet tall (this I found out later), and turning very slowly. Out in front stood a tightly muscled guy in faded jeans, balding suede boots splotched with grease, and a strap-style tee shirt. He wore a derby hat tilted on his coal-black hair. A filterless cigarette was parked behind one ear. He looked like a cartoon carnival barker from an old-time newspaper strip. There was an open toolbox and a big portable radio on an orange crate beside him. The Faces were singing "Stay with Me." The guy was bopping to the beat, hands in his back pockets, hips moving side to side. I had a thought, absurd but perfectly clear: *When I grow up, I want to look just like this guy*.

He pointed to the pass. "Freddy Dean sent you, right? Told you everything else was closed, but you could take a ride on the big wheel."

"Yes, sir."

"A ride on the Spin means you're in. He likes the chosen few to get the aerial view. You gonna take the job?"

"I think so."

He stuck out his hand. "I'm Lane Hardy. Welcome aboard, kid."

I shook with him. "Devin Jones."

"Pleased to meet you."

He started up the inclined walk leading to the gently turning ride, grabbed a long lever that looked like a stick shift, and edged it back. The wheel came to a slow stop with one of the gaily painted cabins (the image of Howie the Happy Hound on each) swaying at the passenger loading dock.

"Climb aboard, Jonesy. I'm going to send you up where the air is rare and the view is much more than fair."

I climbed into the cabin and closed the door. Lane gave it a shake to make sure it was latched, dropped the safety bar, then returned to his rudimentary controls. "Ready for takeoff, cap'n?"

"I guess so."

"Amazement awaits." He gave me a wink and advanced the control stick. The wheel began to turn again and all at once he was looking up at me. So was the old lady by the fortune-telling booth. Her neck was craned and she was shading her eyes. I waved to her. She didn't wave back.

Then I was above everything but the convoluted dips and twists of the Thunderball, rising into the chilly early spring air, and feeling—stupid but true—that I was leaving all my cares and worries down below.

Joyland wasn't a theme park, which allowed it to have a little bit of everything. There was a secondary roller coaster called the Delirium Shaker and a water slide (Captain Nemo's Splash & Crash). On the far western side of the park was a special annex for the little ones called the Wiggle-Waggle Village. There was also a concert hall where most of the acts—this I also learned later—were either B-list C&W or the kind of rockers who peaked in the fifties or sixties. I remember that Johnny Otis and Big Joe Turner did a show there together. I had to ask Brenda Rafferty, the head accountant who was also a kind of den mother to the Hollywood Girls, who they were. Bren thought I was dense; I thought she was old; we were both probably right.

Lane Hardy took me all the way to the top and then stopped the wheel. I sat in the swaying car, gripping the

safety bar, and looking out at a brand-new world. To the
west was the North Carolina flatland, looking incredibly
green to a New England kid who was used to thinking of
March as nothing but true spring's cold and muddy pre-
cursor. To the east was the ocean, a deep metallic blue
until it broke in creamy-white pulses on the beach where I
would tote my abused heart up and down a few months
hence. Directly below me was the good-natured jumble of
Joyland—the big rides and small ones, the concert hall and
concessions, the souvenir shops and the Happy Hound
Shuttle, which took customers to the adjacent motels and,
of course, the beach. To the north was Heaven's Bay. From
high above the park (upstairs, where the air is rare), the town
looked like a nestle of children's blocks from which four
church steeples rose at the major points of the compass.

The wheel began to move again. I came down feeling
like a kid in a Rudyard Kipling story, riding on the nose of
an elephant. Lane Hardy brought me to a stop, but didn't
bother to unlatch the car's door for me; I was, after all,
almost an employee.

"How'd you like it?"

"Great," I said.

"Yeah, it ain't bad for a grandma ride." He reset his derby
so it slanted the other way and cast an appraising eye over
me. "How tall are you? Six-three?"

"Six-four."

"Uh-huh. Let's see how you like ridin all six-four of you
on the Spin in the middle of July, wearin the fur and singin
'Happy Birthday' to some spoiled-rotten little snothole with

cotton candy in one hand and a meltin Kollie Kone in the other."

"Wearing what fur?"

But he was headed back to his machinery and didn't answer. Maybe he couldn't hear me over his radio, which was now blasting "Crocodile Rock." Or maybe he just wanted my future occupation as one of Joyland's cadre of Happy Hounds to come as a surprise.

♥

I had over an hour to kill before meeting with Fred Dean again, so I strolled up Hound Dog Way toward a lunch-wagon that looked like it was doing a pretty good business. Not everything at Joyland was canine-themed, but plenty of stuff was, including this particular eatery, which was called Pup-A-Licious. I was on a ridiculously tight budget for this little job-hunting expedition, but I thought I could afford a couple of bucks for a chili-dog and a paper cup of French fries.

When I reached the palm-reading concession, Madame Fortuna planted herself in my path. Except that's not quite right, because she was only Fortuna between May fifteenth and Labor Day. During those sixteen weeks, she dressed in long skirts, gauzy, layered blouses, and shawls decorated with various cabalistic symbols. Gold hoops hung from her ears, so heavy they dragged the lobes down, and she talked in a thick Romany accent that made her sound like a character from a 1930s fright-flick, the kind featuring mist-shrouded castles and howling wolves.

During the rest of the year she was a widow from Brooklyn who collected Hummel figures and liked movies (especially the weepy-ass kind where some chick gets cancer and dies beautifully). Today she was smartly put together in a black pantsuit and low heels. A rose-pink scarf around her throat added a touch of color. As Fortuna, she sported masses of wild gray locks, but that was a wig, and still stored under its own glass dome in her little Heaven's Bay house. Her actual hair was a cropped cap of dyed black. The *Love Story* fan from Brooklyn and Fortuna the Seer only came together in one respect: both fancied themselves psychic.

"There is a shadow over you, young man," she announced.

I looked down and saw she was absolutely right. I was standing in the shadow of the Carolina Spin. We both were.

"Not that, stupidnik. Over your future. You will have a hunger."

I had a bad one already, but a Pup-A-Licious footlong would soon take care of it. "That's very interesting, Mrs… um…"

"Rosalind Gold," she said, holding out her hand. "But you can call me Rozzie. Everyone does. But during the season…" She fell into character, which meant she sounded like Bela Lugosi with breasts. "Doorink the season, I am… *Fortuna!*"

I shook with her. If she'd been in costume as well as in character, half a dozen gold bangles would have clattered on her wrist. "Very nice to meet you." And, trying on the same accent: "I am… *Devin!*"

She wasn't amused. "An Irish name?"

"Right."

"The Irish are full of sorrow, and many have the sight. I don't know if you do, but you will meet someone who does."

Actually, I was full of happiness…along with that surpassing desire to put a Pup-A-Licious pup, preferably loaded with chili, down my throat. This was feeling like an adventure. I told myself I'd probably feel less that way when I was swabbing out toilets at the end of a busy day, or cleaning puke from the seats of the Whirly Cups, but just then everything seemed perfect.

"Are you practicing your act?"

She drew herself up to her full height, which might have been five-two. "Is no act, my lad." She said *ect* for *act*. "Jews are the most psychically sensitive race on earth. This is a thing everyone knows." She dropped the accent. "Also, Joyland beats hanging out a palmistry shingle on Second Avenue. Sorrowful or not, I like you. You give off good vibrations."

"One of my very favorite Beach Boys songs."

"But you are on the edge of great sorrow." She paused, doing the old emphasis thing. "And, perhaps, danger."

"Do you see a beautiful woman with dark hair in my future?" Wendy was a beautiful woman with dark hair.

"No," Rozzie said, and what came next stopped me dead. "She is in your past."

Ohh-kay.

I walked around her in the direction of Pup-A-Licious, being careful not to touch her. She was a charlatan, I didn't have a single doubt about that, but touching her just then still seemed like a lousy idea.

No good. She walked with me. "In your future is a little girl and a little boy. The boy has a dog."

"A Happy Hound, I bet. Probably named Howie."

She ignored this latest attempt at levity. "The girl wears a red hat and carries a doll. One of these children has the sight. I don't know which. It is hidden from me."

I hardly heard that part of her spiel. I was thinking of the previous pronouncement, made in a flat Brooklyn accent: *She is in your past.*

Madame Fortuna got a lot of stuff wrong, I found out, but she *did* seem to have a genuine psychic touch, and on the day I interviewed for a summer at Joyland, she was hitting on all cylinders...

*Read the rest today!*
*JOYLAND is available now*
*from your favorite bookseller.*
*For more information, visit*
**www.HardCaseCrime.com**

## The Best in Graphic Novels From
## HARD CASE CRIME!

The finest writers and artists team up to tell
searing crime stories in the visual medium:

# Peepland
## by CHRISTA FAUST &
## GARY PHILLIPS

In seedy, sordid 1980s Times Square, a peepshow performer
finds evidence of a murder committed by the son of a wealthy
real estate developer. But will she live to tell the tale?

# Normandy Gold
## by MEGAN ABBOTT &
## ALISON GAYLIN

A small-town sheriff comes to Washington, D.C. to investigate
her sister's disappearance and winds up deep undercover in the
world of politicians, call girls, and the deadliest of dirty tricks.

# Quarry's War
## by MAX ALLAN COLLINS

Once a Marine sniper in Vietnam, Quarry came home to find his
wife cheating on him and no work for a man whose only job skill
was killing. Enter the Broker, an agent for professional hit men.
But when the Broker assigns Quarry to kill a former platoon
mate, will Quarry carry out the contract or fall prey to an attack
of conscience? From the author of *Road to Perdition*, one of
the most acclaimed graphic novels of all time.